Royal House of Corinthia

Royally wed...by Christmas!

This Christmas, Princess Arianna and
Crown Prince Armando of Corinthia are
facing the biggest challenges of their lives.

Pregnant Arianna flees to New York to find some
privacy...only to find her very own Prince Charming!

Christmas Baby for the Princess
Available now

Crown Prince Armando needs a royal bride,
so why can't he stop thinking about his assistant,
Rosa Lamberti?

Winter Wedding for the Prince
Available now

You won't want to miss this delightfully
emotional new duet from Barbara Wallace,
brimming with Christmas magic!

Dear Reader,

Welcome back to Corinthia!

Seems our tiny Mediterranean country has developed a case of wedding fever this holiday season. For starters, Princess Arianna will be marrying her American prince on Christmas Eve. That's not all, however... Rumor has it Crown Prince Armando will be announcing his engagement to the sultan of Yelgiers's daughter on New Year's Day!

The marriage is more strategic alliance than romance, but Prince Armando doesn't mind. He's already married—and lost—the love of his life, and is positive he'll never love again. An arranged marriage with his economic ally solves a multitude of problems, including producing an heir and protecting the country from potential scandal.

There's only one small hitch to his plans: a mistletoe kiss he shared with his assistant, Rosa, has him unable to think of anything else. Could it be that the heart he thought was dead has returned to life at the worst possible time?

What's a prince to do when he's trapped between love and responsibility?

I had fun creating the Royal Family of Corinthia and helping them celebrate Christmas. So much so, in fact, that I'm considering a return next holiday season. If you'd like to see more of these characters, please drop me a line at Barbara@Barbarawallace.com and let me know.

Meanwhile, if you haven't read Princess Arianna's story, you can catch up with last month's *Christmas Baby for the Princess*.

I hope every one of you has a wonderful holiday season. Merry Christmas and happy 2017!

Barbara Wallace

Winter Wedding for the Prince

Barbara Wallace

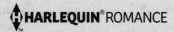

Recycling programs
for this product may
not exist in your area.

ISBN-13: 978-0-373-74412-1

Winter Wedding for the Prince

First North American Publication 2016

Copyright © 2016 by Barbara Wallace

Printed in U.S.A.

Barbara Wallace can't remember when she wasn't dreaming up love stories in her head, so writing romances for Harlequin Romance is a dream come true. Happily married to her own Prince Charming, she lives in New England with a house full of empty-nest animals. Occasionally her son comes home, as well.

To stay up-to-date on Barbara's news and releases, sign up for her newsletter at barbarawallace.com.

Books by Barbara Wallace

Harlequin Romance

Royal House of Corinthia

Christmas Baby for the Princess

The Vineyards of Calanetti

Saved by the CEO

In Love with the Boss

A Millionaire for Cinderella
Beauty & Her Billionaire Boss

The Billionaire's Fair Lady
The Courage to Say Yes
The Man Behind the Mask
Swept Away by the Tycoon
The Unexpected Honeymoon

Visit the Author Profile page
at Harlequin.com for more titles.

For Second Lieutenant Andrew Wallace,
who commissioned five days after I typed
The End. Merry Christmas!

CHAPTER ONE

"Then, after the children finish their sing-along, Babbo Natale will arrive to distribute presents. We were lucky enough this year to get each child something from their wish lists, even the girl who asked for a dragon and one thousand chocolate cookies. The internet is a wonderful thing." Rosa Lamberti looked up from her paperwork. "Are you even listening?" she asked the man in front of her.

Armando Santoro, crown prince of Corinthia, paused midstep to give her a narrow-eyed look. "Of course I did. Babbo Natale. Dragons. Cookies. Why do you ask?"

"I don't know, maybe because you have been wearing a path in the carpet for the past thirty minutes." Pacing like a caged panther was more like it. He had been crossing the hand-woven Oushak with long, heavy-footed strides that took advantage of his extra-tall frame. Between that and the scowl plastered on his face, she half expected him to start growling. "I have a feeling I could have announced a coup and you wouldn't have heard me."

"I'm sorry," he said, running a hand through his dark curls. "I'm a bit distracted this morning."

Clearly. Setting her paperwork aside, Rosa helped herself to a fresh cup of coffee. On good days, being the prince's personal assistant was a three-cup job. When he was distracted, the number increased to four or five.

"Don't tell me you're upset about your sister," she said. Only that morning, Princess Arianna had announced her engagement to an American businessman named Max Brown whom she had met in New York City. The details of the courtship were sketchy. According to Armando, the princess had taken off for America without a word why. A few days after her return, Max Brown forced his way into the castle demanding to see her. The pair had been inseparable ever since.

"No," he said. It was more a sigh than reply. "If Arianna is happy, then I am happy for her."

Happy was too mild a term. Rosa would go with delirious or ecstatic. The princess had lit up like Corinthia City on San Paolo Day when Max burst through the door.

Rosa suppressed a sigh of her own. Wild, passionate declarations of love and sudden engagements. It was all quite romantic. She couldn't remember the last time a man declared anything to her, unless you counted her ex-husband and his many declarations of disinterest.

Fredo had been very good at telling her she wasn't worth his time.

She returned to the question at hand. "If it is not your sister, then what is it?" she asked over the rim of her coffee cup. "And don't say nothing, because I know you." One didn't spend seven years of life attached to someone—four as a sister-in-law—without learning a person's tics.

An olive-skinned hand reached over her

shoulder and took the cup before her lips had a chance to make contact. "Hey!"

Turning, she saw Armando already drinking. "You forgot the sugar," he said with a frown.

"I forgot nothing." What little was left of the warm liquid splashed against the rim as she snatched the cup free. "I'm on a diet."

"You're always on a diet. A teaspoon or two of sugar will not kill you."

Said the god of athleticism. He wasn't in danger of finishing out the year a dress size larger. Even sitting perfectly straight, she swore she could feel the button on her waistband threatening to pop.

Sucking in her belly, she said, "Stop trying to change the subject. I asked you a question."

"Did you just demand I answer you? I'm sorry, I was under the impression that you worked for me."

"Yes, but I'm family. That gives me special privileges."

"Like bossiness?"

"I'm not the one ruining a one-hundred-and-fifty-year-old rug." Reaching for the coffeepot, she poured him a fresh coffee of his own, making sure to add the two sugars before refilling her cup. "Seriously, Armando. What's wrong?"

This sigh was the loudest of the three. Taking the coffee, he came around to the front of the love seat and sat down beside her. Rosa did her best to squeeze into the corner to accommodate him. She didn't know if her brother-in-law kept forgetting she wasn't as petite as his late wife or what, but he always insisted on invading her personal space rather than taking a seat across the way. As a result, they sat wedged together, their thighs pressed tight. Rosa gave a silent thank-you for long jackets. It provided another layer between their bodies.

Oblivious, as usual, to the close quarters, Armando stared at the coffee she'd handed him. "Arianna's pregnant," he said in a dull voice.

No wonder they were rushing the engagement. "But that's a good thing, isn't it?" she asked. "Your father finally has another heir to the throne." It was no secret the king was eager to establish a third generation of Santoros to protect his family's legacy.

"It would be," Armando replied, "if Max Brown were the father."

"What?" Rosa's hand froze mid-sip. She would ask if he was joking, except this wasn't something to joke about. "Who…?" It didn't matter. "Does Max know?"

"Yes, and he doesn't care."

"He must love your sister very much." Took a special kind of love to marry a woman carrying another man's child. Certainly not the kind of love people like Rosa got to witness. People like her got a leftover kind of love. As Fredo had been so fond of telling her, she was flavorless and bland.

"Max's devotion is wonderful for Arianna, but…"

But it didn't erase the problems this pregnancy caused. "He or she can't be the heir."

Corinthian law stated that only the biological offspring of both parents could inherit the throne. Should anything happen to Armando and Arianna, then the title would skip to someone else, such as Arianna and

Max's child or one of the distant cousins. Either way opened a host of complications.

"Not to mention that if the truth were to come out, that child would spend the rest of his or her life hounded by gossip and innuendo. Max and Arianna, too. The whole house of Santoro, for that matter."

"Unless Arianna and Max lie." Armando scowled at her suggestion. "What?" she asked. "You don't think that's happened before?" Not even the house of Santoro was that lily pure. In fact, someone trying to slip an illegitimate heir into the mix was probably the reason for the inane law to begin with.

"Whether it's been done before or not isn't the point," he replied. "Other generations didn't have tabloids or your wonderful internet."

Good point. Today, secrets couldn't last forever. Eventually the truth would come out, and when it did, there would be challenges. Corinthia would be plunged into a protracted legal battle that benefited no one.

"I take it you've already thought of trying to change the law," she said.

"Of course, but again, this isn't the old days, when the king could change the laws on a whim. The ministers would want to know the reason for the change."

"All hail increased democracy," Rosa muttered. There wasn't much more that could be done, barring Armando remarrying and having children of his own, and a monk dated more than he did. The Melancholy Prince, the papers called him. The title fit. While Armando had always been serious, Christina's death had added an extra layer. It was as though he was suspended in permanent mourning. He never attended anything that wasn't an official event, and those he attended alone. Other than his sister, Rosa was the only woman in his life.

The prince had returned his attention to his coffee, studying the untouched contents from beneath thick lashes as if they contained the answer. Rosa couldn't help but indulge in a moment of appreciation. If he decided to date again, Armando's return to the dating world would be a welcome one. Even if he wasn't the future king of Corinthia, he was a man worthy of desire.

Granted, he wasn't the most beautiful man in the country; his Roman features were a little too pronounced, although not so much that they looked out of proportion. Besides, she always thought a strong man should have strong features. Fredo, for all his self-importance, had had a weak chin.

The muscles in Armando's chin twitched with tension.

"You know King El Halwani," he started.

"That's a silly question." Of course she knew the man. The sultan of Yelgiers was a frequent visitor. Corinthia and the tiny principality had a long history of economic and political relations. "What does he have to do with anything?"

"His daughter, Mona, is of marrying age."

"Is that so? I didn't know." Rosa's insides ran cold. Surely, he wasn't…

"A union between our two countries will be a tremendous alliance."

Did he say will? The chill spread down her spine, ending in a shiver.

Apology darkened his eyes to near black. "I called him this morning and suggested we discuss an arrangement."

"You—you did." Rosa set down her cup. The coffee she'd been drinking threatened to rise back up her throat.

Armando, remarrying.

She shouldn't have been surprised. Royalty lived a different kind of life than commoners like her. Marriages were arranged for all kinds of reasons: trade relations, military alliances. Why not to secure an heir?

The news still made her queasy. It was too quick. Armando wasn't the type to make rash decisions. For crying out loud, he'd waited a year before proposing to her sister, and they'd fallen in love at first sight. For him to wake up and decide he was going to marry a virtual stranger was completely out of character, looming scandal or no looming scandal. At the very least, he would have asked her what she thought.

But he hadn't. He hadn't sought her opinion at all. So much for being his right hand. Apparently the familiarity she thought they had developed over the past three years had been in her head.

She forced a smile. Pretended she was excited for his news. "I'm sure the people of Corinthia will be thrilled. As will your father."

"I'm not doing this for my father," he replied.

"I know. You're doing it to protect your sister."

"No, I'm doing it for Corinthia." His voice was sharp, the way it always was when his will was questioned. "I'm first in line. It is my responsibility to do whatever I can to ensure Corinthia has a long and peaceful future."

"Of course. I'm sorry." If there was anything Armando took seriously, it was his duty to his country.

Leaving Armando, she stood and walked toward the windows. The crown prince's suite overlooked the south lawn. The famed topiary menagerie remained green, but the grass had gone brown from the winter, and the flowerbeds were empty. Across the street, a pair of business owners were filling their outside window boxes with fresh evergreen—a Corinthian Christmas tradition. When they finished, a single white candle would be placed in the center, another tradition. Greens for life, light for the blessings of the future.

Apparently, Armando's future involved a bride.

What did that mean for her future then? For three years, it had been the two of them, prince and assistant, tied together as they both began lives without their spouses. Being there to help Armando had given her strength and purpose. She'd been able to rebuild the layers of self-esteem Fredo had destroyed.

What now? A new queen would mean new staff, new routines. Would she even have a place in Armando's life anymore? The grip on her chest squeezed tighter.

She watched as a *merli* poked at the barren grass looking for seeds. Poor little creature wasn't having much luck. She could identify. She felt a little like she'd been left wanting, too.

The thing was, she had always known there was the chance Armando would move on with his life. The news shouldn't be this disconcerting.

Then again, he should have told her. They

were supposed to be friends. Family. They'd held hands at her sister's bedside and cried together. She let him drink her coffee, for God's sake. Why hadn't he told her?

"When are you making the announcement?" she asked. It would have to be soon if Armando wanted to draw attention from his sister. Depending upon how far along in her pregnancy Arianna had been when she met Max last month, there was a good chance the princess would start to show soon.

Behind her, she heard the soft clap of a cup against the coffee table, but she didn't turn around.

"We're making the formal announcement on New Year's Day."

What? When she thought soon, she didn't mean that soon. No wonder she couldn't breathe. In three and a half weeks, everything she'd come to know and rely on was going to change forever.

"Is everything all right?" she heard him ask.

"Of course," she lied. "Why wouldn't it be?"

"It truly is the best solution."

"I know." He had no reason to defend himself any more than she had the right to be upset.

Clearly, that didn't stop either of them from doing so anyway.

She was upset with him. Armando could tell because when she spoke, every third or fourth word had an upward inflection. Not that he was surprised. From the moment he made his decision, he'd worried she might see his remarrying as betraying her sister.

Staring at her back, he wished he knew what she was thinking. But then, she was good at hiding behind things. Her poker face was among the best.

"You know that if there was any other way…" he said.

"I know."

Did she? Did she know he'd been up half the night weighing options, or that, given his druthers, he would never remarry? He'd had his chance at love. Four wonderful years with the girl of his dreams. If the price for those years was spending the rest of his life in solitude, he'd been prepared. He didn't mind. After all, if he needed a companion, he had Rosa. She was better company than any consort might be.

Unfortunately, for men like him, what he wanted didn't always matter. The mantle of responsibility outweighed personal desire every time.

Leaving his coffee behind, he joined her at the window. "Corinthia's almost ready for the holiday," he said, noting the men arranging greenery outside. "They'll be lighting the candles tonight."

Rosa didn't answer. She stood with her hands clasped tightly behind her back, stiff and formal, like a proper royal servant, a pose she usually only struck in public. Armando didn't like it. He preferred the relaxed, irreverent Rosa who kept him on his toes and saved him from drowning in his grief.

After Christina died, he'd wanted to die, too. What good was living if his heart lay six feet underground? Rosa had been the only one who had been able to break through the darkness that filled his soul. She needed him, she'd claimed, to help her rebuild fol-

lowing her divorce. It was a lie, of course—
Rosa was one of the strongest women he
knew—but he let her think he believed the
excuse. Helping her find a lawyer and place
to live gave him a reason to drag himself
out of bed that first day. Then, when she
became his assistant, there were meetings
and charitable initiatives and other projects
she insisted needed his attention, and so he
continued dragging himself out of bed. Until
the day came when getting up was no longer a trial.

She'd kept him tied to the land of the living, Rosa did. Without her, he would still be
lost in his grief. Or rather, lost even deeper.

Which was why he needed her support
now.

"You never met my grandfather, did you?"

"King Damian? No." She wasn't so annoyed that she couldn't give him a side-eyed
look. Of course she hadn't met the man. Illness forced him off the throne before Armando was born.

"He came upstairs to my room one night,
a few weeks before he died, and got me out
of bed so I could see what it looked like with

candles lit in every window. I must have been seven or eight at the time. Corinthia City wasn't as developed as it is now. Anyway, he told me how all those candles represented Corinthians hoping for the future. 'One day you will be responsible for those candles,' he told me. 'It will be up to you to keep them burning bright.' I never forgot." The words were the weight pressing on his shoulders every time he saw a candle flickering.

He turned to look at his sister-in-law. "Father's aging, Rosa. I could see it this past month when Arianna disappeared. He's never truly gotten over Mama's death…" He paused to let the irony of his words settle between them. The curse of the Santoro men: to live a lifetime of grieving. "And I think he would like to step down, but he's afraid for the future. It's important he know that as his successor, I am willing to do whatever it takes to keep those lights burning."

"Including political marriage."

He shrugged. "Ours won't be the first royal marriage based on obligation rather than love." If anything, a man in his position was lucky to have spent four years with a wife he did love. "It would be nice, however, to know I have my best friend's support. Do I?"

The clock on the nearby mantel ticked off the seconds while he waited for her response. Unfortunately, her eyes were cast downward. They were the one feature that couldn't mask her feelings. In that way, she was like her sister. Christina had also had expressive brown eyes. Beyond their eyes, however, the two were dramatically different. Christina had been all passion and energy, with a beauty that commanded attention. Rosa was softer. Whereas Christina was bright like a star, her sister was more the glow of a candle.

Finally, her shoulders relaxed. "Of course you have my blessing," she said. "You know I can never say no to you."

Armando's shoulders relaxed in turn. "I know. It's my charm."

"No, it's because you're going to be king. I say no and you might have me thrown in the dungeon."

"As one does." He relaxed a little more.

Rosa making jokes was always a good sign. "I'm serious, Rosa. Your support is important to me." Just thinking he might not have it had left a tight knot in the center of his chest.

A hand brushed his arm. Initiating contact with a member of the royal family was considered a violation of protocol, but he and Rosa had been together too long for either of them to care about rules. There were times, in fact, when he found her touch comforting. Like now, the way her fingertips seemed to brush the tension from his muscles. "You have it. Seriously. I just wish…"

"What?"

She shook her head. "Nothing. I'm being silly. You have my support, 'Mando."

"Good." Although he wondered what she had started to say. That she wished there didn't have to be a wedding? If so, Armando agreed.

But there was going to be a wedding, and he was glad to have his best friend's support.

Hopefully, she wouldn't change her mind when she heard his next request.

CHAPTER TWO

"I CANNOT BELIEVE you want me to attend a meeting with you and your future father-in-law. How is that possibly in good form?"

She had been complaining since yesterday. When he'd said he'd called King Omar, Armando left off that the sultan was in Corinthia and that they were going to meet for lunch the next day.

"And how is it no one was told of his visit?" she asked as they rode the elevator down to the first floor. "He's a visiting head of state. There are protocols to be followed."

"Since when do you follow protocol?"

"I always follow protocol when other royalty is involved. Exactly how long has he been in Corinthia?"

"Since Wednesday. You might as well get used to it," he added when she opened her mouth to speak. "Omar has decided to personally oversee the resort development." Such was the major difference between the two small countries. The Yelgierian royal family insisted on maintaining control of everything, while Armando and his father preferred giving their subjects more freedom. "Between that and the upcoming…arrangement…" He couldn't bring himself to say the word *wedding*. Not yet. "I suspect Omar will be going back and forth quite a bit."

An odd looking shadow crossed her face. "With his daughter?"

"I—I don't know." Armando hadn't given his bride-to-be much thought. "I imagine she will, considering all the preparations that need to take place."

"Unless the wedding is in Yelgiers," Rosa replied. She was studying her shoes as she spoke, so he almost didn't hear her.

"True." He hadn't given much thought to logistics. Those kinds of details were usually up to the bride. "But it doesn't matter to me where the wedding takes place." Only that it did, and Corinthia's future was secure.

The elevator opened, and they stepped out

into the guarded enclave near the driveway. Rosa's sedan had been brought around and sat running by the curb.

"I still don't understand why you need me for this meeting," she said as a guard stepped out to open the passenger door. "Surely, you can finalize your—" she glanced at the guard "—agreement without me."

"I told you, this meeting isn't about my 'agreement,'" Armando replied. "I'm meeting with him to discuss the development project." And perhaps finalize a few details regarding yesterday's telephone conversation. Sometimes she was a little too astute for his liking. "You know I like to have you with me when I discuss business."

He waited until the guard shut her door and they once again had privacy. "Not to mention you are my favorite driver." The way Rosa handled a car made him feel comfortable. For a long time, just the thought of being on the road filled him with dread. He would hear the sound of an engine, and images of twisted steel filled his brain. But, just like she coaxed him back to the land of the living, Rosa had eased him onto the road.

Sometimes he wondered what his life would be like without her.

"So now I'm your driver," she replied. "If that's the case, maybe I should get a cap to wear."

"And have me listen to you complain about the hat ruining your hair? No, thank you. What you're wearing will suffice."

For a meeting she didn't want to attend, she was dressed rather nicely. As usual, her brown hair was pulled up in one of those twisty, formal styles she seemed to prefer, but unlike her usual skirt and blouse, she had on a brocade dress with matching jacket. A long one that seemed designed to hide a woman's shape. She wore those a lot—long, bulky jackets, that was. He wasn't a fan. It was as though she was trying to discourage attention.

"When's the last time you had a date?" he asked her.

For the first time he could remember, she stripped the car gears. Turning her head, she squinted at him. "Excuse me?"

The question did sound like it came out of nowhere. It was just that looking at her, and thinking about how she continually hid her assets, had him curious. "I was wondering when was the last time you had been on a date."

"Why do you want to know?"

"No particular reason. Only that it dawned on me that I can't remember the last time you mentioned one."

This time she downshifted smoothly. "My being silent doesn't have to mean I'm not dating. How do you know I'm not simply being discreet?"

"Are you? Being discreet, that is." The thought that she might be seeing someone and had not said anything irritated him. At the same time, he found it hard to believe a woman as attractive as Rosa didn't have offers.

"Isn't that a bit personal?" she asked him. "It's called a private life for a reason."

"Yes, but you can tell me—we're friends."

His comment earned him a sharp laugh. "You mean like you told me about your plans to get married?"

"I did tell you."

"After the fact."

What was she talking about? "You were the first person I told."

The car slowed as she looked at him again. "I was?"

"Of course." He thought she knew that. "I told you how much your support meant to me."

"I know, but I didn't think…" Was that pink creeping into her cheeks? It was hard to tell, the driver's side being in shadow. "I'm sorry I snapped."

"I am sorry for prying. It was rude of me." He still would like to know, however. It was protectiveness as much as curiosity. To make sure she chose better this time around. While he didn't know much about her marriage, beyond the fact it had ended badly, he did know her ex enough to dislike him. Back when Christina was alive, Fredo and Rosa had attended a handful of state dinners. Armando found the man to be a narcissistic bore. He'd decided the man had to be a closet romantic or something, because how else could he have won a woman as soft and gentle as Rosa?

Then again, maybe Armando's first impression was right, since she'd divorced him. That Rosa, for her part, refused to talk about the man said as much.

"The answer is no," Rosa said, shaking him from his thoughts. "I'm not dating."

"At all?" He wasn't sure why he felt relieved at her answer. Perhaps because he feared a serious relationship might cause her to leave her job. "Surely you've had offers, though."

Again, she gave a strange laugh, although this one had less bite than the other. "Not as many as you would think. In case you didn't realize, my job eats up most of my time."

Was that truly the reason? The undercurrent in her laugh made him wonder. "Is that your way of hinting you need time off?" he asked. If so, it would be the first. Usually she had no trouble speaking up.

Another reason to question the excuse.

Rosa shook her head. "Not at all. At least not right now."

They'd reached the point in the highway where they had to choose whether to take the mountain pass or the longer, more circuitous route. Armando gave a slight smile as she turned onto the longer route. By mutual agreement, they hadn't driven the mountain road in three years. Feeling a warmth spreading across his chest, he reached over and gave her hand a grateful squeeze. Her eyes widened a little, but she smiled nonetheless.

"The truth is," she said, after he'd lifted his hand, "I haven't had a lot of interest in dating. I'm still working on getting to know myself again."

What an odd thing to say. Then again, maybe it wasn't so odd. Certainly he wasn't the same man following Christina's death, the hole caused by her absence impossible to repair. No doubt, Rosa's divorce left a similar wound.

She'd also lost a sibling. Sometimes, in his selfishness, he forgot that Rosa had suffered as much loss as he had. The idea that she might have been hurting as bad as he made his conscience sting that much more.

"Aren't we a pair," he mused out loud. "Three years removed, and we're still struggling to move forward without our spouses. What do you think that says about us?"

"Well, in your case, I'd say it's because you have a singular heart."

"I would think the same could be said for you."

"Hardly," she replied with a bark. "Do not insult my sister by even mentioning our marriages in the same breath. Fredo isn't fit to carry Christina's water."

On that they agreed, but to hear her say so with such forcefulness surprised him nevertheless. Usually when the topic of her former husband came up, she pretended the man didn't exist.

"What did he do to you? Fredo," he asked. Had he been unfaithful? Armando couldn't believe anyone married to Rosa would want to stray, but Fredo was a boor.

She shot him a look before changing lanes. "Who says Fredo did anything?"

The defensiveness in her tone. "Did he?"

"Water under the bridge," was her only reply. "My marriage is over, and I'm better off for it. Let's just leave things at that."

"Fine." Today wasn't the day to press for details and start an argument. That didn't mean he wasn't still curious, however, or that he wouldn't try again another time.

Rosa kept one eye on the rearview mirror as she moved from lane to lane. What had she been thinking bringing Fredo's name into the mix in the first place? Her marriage—or rather, her role in it—was her greatest shame; she would rather pretend it never happened than admit her own pathetic behavior. Especially to Armando, whose pain and loss far outweighed hers. To hear him now, trying to equate the two…

At least he'd agreed to change the subject. Hopefully telling him she was working on herself satisfied enough of his curiosity. After all, it wasn't as though she was lying. She *was* rediscovering herself. Learning, little by little, that there was a capable woman inside her chubby shell. As her therapist one reminded, her value went beyond being her husband's verbal whipping post. And, while she was still a work in progress, she had begun to like herself again.

There were days, of course, when Fredo's insults haunted her, but his voice, once so prominent in her ear, was growing softer. If she learned anything from Christina's death, it was that life was too short to settle for anything, or anyone. She'd stupidly let herself believe she had no choice when Fredo proposed. Never again. She realized now that she deserved nothing less than unconditional love. Next time, if there was a next time, she wouldn't settle for anything less. There would be no settling the next time around. She wanted someone who loved her body and soul. Who made her heart flutter whenever she heard his voice, and whose heart fluttered in return.

She wanted what Armando had with Christina.

What he would eventually have with his bride-to-be. Sure, Armando's marriage might begin for political reasons, but time had a way of warming a person's heart, especially if the person deserved to be loved. Rosa had done some internet searching last night, and discovered Mona El Halwani was a caramel-skinned beauty whose statuesque body weighed at least forty pounds less than

Rosa's. She was exquisite. A walking, talking advertisement for perfection.

How could Armando's heart not warm to perfection?

They left the city behind. The landscape around them began to change revealing more and more of Corinthia's old-world. Stone farmhouses lined the streets, their window boxes stuffed with fresh greens.

Seeing the candles in the windows, Rosa couldn't help but think of what Armando had said about being responsible for every light in every window. Such a heavy weight to grow up bearing—the future of your country on your shoulders. She suddenly wanted to pull over, wrap him in a hug and let him know he didn't have to bear the burden alone.

As if those words coming from her would mean anything. Providing solace was his future wife's job. Not hers. She might as well get used to the new hierarchy right now and just do her job.

An hour later, they arrived at the Cerulean Towers, the luxury high-rise that housed

Yelgiers's development concern. It was as unheralded an arrival as King Omar's, with only the doorman to greet them.

The sultan was waiting for them in his penthouse suite. Tall and exceptionally handsome, he greeted Armando with the very type of embrace Rosa had considered earlier. "I have been awaiting this moment since yesterday's phone conversation," he said, clapping Armando on the back. "That our families will be forever joined warms my heart."

Rosa stifled a giggle as she watched Armando, clearly caught off guard by the effusiveness, awkwardly pat the man in return. His cheeks were crimson. "You honor me, Omar."

"On the contrary, it is you who honor my family by taking Mona as your bride. Your union marks the beginning of a long and fruitful alliance between our countries."

"Your enthusiasm humbles me," Armando replied as he disentangled himself. "My father sends his regards, by the way, and his welcome."

"Please send my regards in return. Tell

him I look forward to the day he and I toast the birth of our grandson."

Rosa choked on the cough rising in her throat. All the effusiveness was making her insides cringe.

Armando arched his brow at the sound. "You remember my assistant, Rosa Lamberti," he said, motioning to her.

She started to bow only to have her hands swept up in the sultan's large bronze grasp. Apparently, his enthusiasm didn't only apply to Armando. "Of course. A man would never forget a beautiful woman. Especially one whose face makes the flowers weep." As the sultan pressed a kiss to her knuckles, Rosa heard Armando give a cough of his own. She waited until King Omar turned and flashed him a smirk.

He led them inside and to the penthouse dining room. The table, Rosa noticed, had been set with a combination of Yelgierian and Corinthian colors, including a large centerpiece of greens, jasmine and dianthus, the official Yelgierian and Corinthian flowers. Meant to be a tribute to their merging families, the red and gold looked unexpectedly festive as well. There was wine chilling and a trio of uniformed waiters standing at the ready next to the sideboard.

"A working lunch," King Omar explained. "I thought it would be more efficient."

That depended upon your definition of efficient, Rosa thought, counting the silverware. Chances were she would be eating salads for the next week to make up for the excess.

"I am sorry Mona couldn't be here to join us," the king said as the waiters wheeled out the first course, a rich, spicy-smelling soup that had Rosa amending her plans to two weeks of salad. "I called and requested that she fly here this morning, but sadly, she told me she wasn't feeling up to traveling."

"She's not well?" Concern marked Armando's face. Rosa knew what he was thinking. If she was sickly, Mona might not have the stamina to meet the demands that came with being queen.

"The flu," King Omar replied. "Caught during one of her visits to our local children's hospital."

"One of?" Rosa asked.

"She spends a great deal of time there. Children's charities are among her passions. In fact, she recently completed her degree in children's psychology."

"Impressive," Armando replied.

"Public service is a duty our family takes quite seriously. We understand the responsibility that comes with power. Although of all my children, I have to say that Mona takes her responsibility the most seriously."

Smart, charitable and, guessing from King Omar's looks, beautiful. Rosa reached for her water to cool the heartburn stuck behind her breastbone. Call her a cynic, but Rosa thought the woman sounded too good to be true. If the glint in Armando's eyes was any indication, however, he was impressed.

"That is good to hear," he said, "as our family is extremely interested in social reform. Sadly, as beautiful as Corinthia is, the country is not without its blemishes. We are as susceptible to the problems of the world as every country. Disease. Drugs. Violence.

We're currently working quite hard to stem the problems of domestic abuse."

"Interesting," King Omar replied. "How so?"

"Being an island country can be detrimental," Armando replied. "If women in trouble cannot afford airfare for themselves and their children, they often feel trapped. It's hard to start over when you're looking over your shoulder."

Omar replied, "Are there not laws in place to protect them?"

"Yes, but laws on the books aren't always enough," Rosa said. She could tell from the widening of the king's eyes he hadn't expected her to speak up over Armando, but as always happened when the subject came up, she couldn't contain herself.

"Many of our villages are small and contain generations of connected families," Armando explained. "Women often fear going to the authorities because of their husbands' connections."

"I see," Omar replied. "You said you are working to change this? How?" Rosa wondered if he was thinking about his own small country with its tribal population.

"We've created a number of programs over the past couple years, but the one we're most proud of is called Christina's Home, which gives women who don't have the resources a place where they can escape."

King Omar frowned. "Are you saying you built a safe house?"

"Yes, although we prefer the term *transitional home*. We provide education, legal services and such to help them start over. Right now, we have one home, but our hope is to eventually have a network of two or three Christina's Homes that can address a variety of transitional needs."

During his explanation, the waiters replaced the soup with a plate of flaky fried pastries and salad of greens and roasted peppers that had Rosa extending her salad fast until after the new year. The sultan picked up one of the pastries and took a healthy bite. "Interesting name, Christina's Homes," he said when he finished chewing. "Named after your late wife?"

Some of the light faded from Armando's eyes. "Yes. One of the qualities that made her so special was the way she cared for the welfare of our people. By naming the shelter program after her, we're honoring her memory twofold. In name and in deed. It was Rosa's idea," he added. "She shares her sister's passion for helping people."

She had heard Armando make the same compliment dozens of times without reaction. Today, however, her stomach fluttered. She felt awkward and exposed.

"My sister always believed in taking action," Rosa said. Whereas she'd needed her sister's death before she found the courage to do anything. Reaching for her glass, Rosa hid her shame behind a long drink of water.

On the other side of the table, she could feel the sultan studying her. "This sounds exactly like the type of work my daughter would want to be involved with. How many families have you helped?" he asked.

"Too many to count," Armando replied. "Some only stay for a night or two while they make arrangements in another part of Europe, while others stay longer. This time of year is among our busiest, as we like to make sure circumstances don't prevent the children from enjoying the magic of the holidays. Every year we host a Christmas party for current and past residents, complete with traditional foods and presents."

"It's also when we host our largest fundraiser," Rosa added. "The Concert for Christina's Home is broadcast nationwide and is fast becoming a tradition." Even though she felt ashamed about her own behavior, she was spectacularly proud of how her sister's legacy had taken hold. All those late nights she and Armando worked, neither of them willing to go home and face their sad empty lives. That the program thrived proved amazing things could come out of even the most profound sadness. It was almost as much of a legacy to their triumph over grief as it was a tribute to Christina.

"The program sounds exactly like the kind of work Mona would want to see continued." Rosa jerked from her thoughts just in time to hear King Omar mention his daughter's involvement. "I have no doubt she would be honored if you allowed her to help expand the work being done in your first wife's name."

Armando would never allow it, she thought as possessiveness took hold. Christina's

Home was too sacred to let a stranger—even one he planned to marry—become involved. She looked across the table, expecting to find him giving her a reassuring look. Instead, she found him taking an unusually long drink of water.

"The people of Corinthia would appreciate that," he said finally. He looked to her, eyes filled with silent apology.

Rosa lost her appetite.

"He backed me into a corner," Armando said when they were on the elevator and heading back downstairs. "It would have been insulting to say anything other than yes."

Rosa didn't reply. Mainly because she didn't want to admit Armando was right. The king had practically forced his daughter's involvement on Armando. That didn't make it sting any less.

Christina's Home had been her idea as a way of honoring her sister. She'd been the one poring over the budget with Armando and massaging corporate donors. What made King Omar think his daughter could waltz in and become Armando's partner?

Because Mona was to be his wife, that's what. Next year at this time, it would be Mona helping Armando. Mona going over party plans in his dimly lit office while he shed his jacket and tie. Letting him drink her coffee when he grew punchy. For a man who could dominate a room of leaders, Armando managed to look like a sleepy cat when tired. So adorably rumpled. She'd bet Mona wouldn't be able to resist running a hand through his curls when she saw him.

Oh, for crying out loud, you'd think she was jealous, worrying what Mona did with Armando's hair. What mattered was maintaining control over a charity she'd helped create.

"Clearly, he thought playing up his daughter's generous nature would impress me," Armando replied. Busy adjusting his jacket, he thankfully missed Rosa's scowl. The man certainly had been eager to paint his daughter in a good light.

"Did it work?" she asked.

"Did what work? Singing his daughter's praises?" He gave his cuff a tug. "I suppose. It's good to know the future queen has a keen understanding of her responsibilities. Although right now King Omar is going out of his way to paint her in the most positive light possible. He's quite a salesman in that regard."

"You think he's exaggerating?" She was ashamed at the thrill she felt over the possibility of a problem.

The shake of Armando's head quickly squelched the notion. "Oh, no, the El Halwani dedication to social causes has been well documented. They are considered among the most progressive ruling families in the region."

Of course they were. No doubt the mythical Mona would be extremely dedicated to bettering Corinthian society, including helping Christina's Home. Next year, she would be the one working by Armando's side. While he left Rosa behind.

She pressed a fist to her midsection. Lunch truly wasn't agreeing with her. What started as a burning sensation had grown to a full-blown knot that stretched from her breast to her throat.

"Do you feel all right?" Armando asked. "You've been pale since lunch."

"Too much spicy food. My stomach wasn't expecting such an exotic lunch."

"Are you sure that's all?" he asked, turning in her direction.

Rosa hated when he studied her like that, like he could read her mind. She could almost feel his blue eyes reaching through her outer layers and into her thoughts. "I—"

The elevator doors opened, saving her from trying to tap-dance in close quarters. Quickly, she stepped out into the lobby. "Why would there be something else?" she asked once she was safely a step or two ahead. "Can't a woman have a problem digesting spices?"

"Of course. She can also be hurt."

How was she supposed to respond to that? What could she say that didn't sound jealous and possessive? "I don't know what you're talking about," she said.

"I think you do." His fingers caught her wrist, stopping her from going farther.

In the center of the lobby stood an indoor fountain, ruled over by a small marble cherub. Maintaining his grasp, Armando tugged her toward the fountain edge, where he took a seat on the marble wall. "I think we should talk," he said, pulling her down next to him. "I know why you're upset, and I understand."

"You do?" Rosa doubted his did. How could he, when she wasn't 100 percent sure why she was reacting so strongly herself.

What she did notice was how the marble beneath them made her more aware of their close position than usual. She could feel Armando's body warmth radiating against her leg, even though the only parts of them touching were his wrist on her hand. And, she realized, looking down, that was no longer true.

Looking up again, she came eye to eye with Armando's gentle expression.

"Christina's Home," he said. "You're worried what will happen if Mona gets involved with the program."

Perhaps he understood after all. "It's just that you and I worked so hard to build something together…"

"Which is why I want you to know that I understand, and I promise—" Rosa gasped as he reached up to cradle her face between his hands "—I will never let anything, or anybody, take away your sister's legacy."

Christina, of course. What had she been thinking? She gave him a smile anyway, since his reassurance was well intentioned.

When he smiled back, an odd squiggling sensation passed through her.

"Good," he said. "I'm glad, because you know how much I would hate for you to be upset."

Smile softening even more, he fanned his thumbs across her cheekbones. "I would be lost without you, you know."

He held her cheeks a beat longer before getting to his feet. "Now that we've settled that, do you feel up to driving?" he asked.

"Absolutely," she replied.

As soon as Armando started toward the front door, however, she pressed her hand to her stomach to quell the odd quivering sensation that had sprung up.

CHAPTER THREE

WHEN ROSA AND ARMANDO first conceived of Christina's Home, they wanted to build a place that the late princess would have built herself. Therefore, the home was a sprawling stone villa set at the end of a gated access road. State-of-the-art security assured residents the privacy and safety they needed to rebuild their lives, while acres of grass and gardens gave their children the chance to be children.

For this year's Christmas party, thanks to local businesses and designers eager to earn a royal blessing, the central dining room had been transformed into a winter wonderland. In addition to the traditional Corinthian red and green window boxes, there were "snow"-covered evergreens lining the walls and animated snowmen with motion detectors that brought them to life. There was even an indoor jungle gym modeled after the ice castle from a famous children's movie. All afternoon long, kids had been laughing as they hurled themselves down the indoor "ice" slide into a pile of fake snow.

Rosa stood at the back of the room, near the partition that blocked the corridor and kept the chaos contained to the single room. Near to her, a giant window looked out on snow-covered mountains, including Mount Cornier, whose winding roads had been Christina's final destination. During his dedication speech, Armando said that the view guaranteed the princess would be forever looking down on her legacy.

Rosa wondered what Christina would think if she knew her older sister had spent the last several days fighting a disturbing awareness when it came to Armando. All of a sudden, it seemed, someone had flipped a switch and she was noticing things about him she'd never noticed before, such as how elegant his fingers looked when gripping a pen or the how the bow in his upper lip made a perfect V. What's worse, each detail came with an intense collection of flutters deep inside her, the source of which was a place long dormant. Why, after all this time, she would suddenly and inexplicably be attracted to the man, she didn't know, but there it was. Nature's way of ensuring her self-esteem didn't get too strong, probably. No worries there. Not with Fredo's voice renting space.

"Next year, we are hiring an actor." The object of her thoughts poked his head around the barricade. Rosa tried not to notice he was clad only in a white T-shirt. "I am making it a royal decree."

"You realize you said the same thing last year," she replied.

"Yes, but this year I mean it."

"You said that last year as well." Along with the year before that, when the official shelter was still being built and they housed families at the Corinthian Arms hotel. "You love playing Babbo Natale and you know it." Interacting with the children under the Christmas tree was one of the few times she saw him truly relax. Not to mention it kept them both from feeling maudlin on a day that was supposed to be joyful.

Armando mumbled something unintelligible. "What?" she whispered.

"I said, then at least get me a better beard next year. This one makes my skin itch."

"Yes, Your Highness."

"Be careful. Mock me and Babbo will put you on the naughty list."

"Oh, goody. Naughty girls get all the good gifts."

"How would you know? Is there something you're not telling me, Signora Rosa?"

"I'll never tell." Rosa immediately clamped her jaw shut. She didn't know what horrified her more, the flutters that took flight at his question or her flirty response. To cover, she made a point of studying her watch dial. "Are you almost ready? I think the natives are getting restless."

"I thought Arianna and Max had them under control." The party was serving as the couple's first official appearance. Currently, the princess was playing carols on the shelter piano while her fiancé led the crowd in a sing-along. He was already proving a people's favorite with his movie-idol looks and exuberant off-key singing.

"They are," she told Armando, "but you know children's attention spans. Especially children who have been gorging on cake and gelato."

"The Christmas cake was delicious, was it not?"

"Mouthwatering," she replied, hoping he didn't notice the catch in her voice. Truth was, she had been more transfixed by the way Armando licked the frosting from his fork.

Their conversation was interrupted by the arrival of the future Prince Max. "I have been asked when Santa might be arriving," he said. "We're running out of Christmas songs. If he doesn't arrive soon, I may have to break out the 1940s standards."

"Please no, not that," Rosa replied. She leaned back to look behind the screen only to find herself inches away from Armando's bearded face.

"Never fear, Babbo Natale is here." He grinned. "Ready to see who has been naughty or nice. Should I start with you,

Signora Rosa, since you seem to think the naughty list is the place to be?"

Too bad she wasn't wearing a beard, if only to hide her warm cheeks. She had to settle for looking down and adjusting the hem of her white sweater. "I'm sure there's much more interesting people on that list than me," she said. "Besides, you don't want to keep the children waiting for their presents much longer or we could have a riot on our hands."

Proving her point, one of the youngsters spotted his red hat poking out from behind the screen. "It's Babbo!" he yelled out. "He's here!" Half a second later, the rest of the children started cheering his arrival as well. The mothers had to corral their children to keep them from rushing the cloth screen.

"Looks like I'm on," Armando whispered. He stepped out, and in the blink of an eye, every trace of reluctance disappeared as the prince threw himself into his performance. "Ho, ho, ho!" he called out. "*Buon Natale!* One of my helpers told me I might find some good boys and girls here. Is that true?"

"Yes," the kids screeched at the top of their lungs.

"Wonderful. Because I happen to have a sack full of toys that I brought especially for them."

Someone dragged over a folding chair from one of the tables, and he perched on it as regally as if it were an actual throne, despite the fact his athletic frame dwarfed the chair. "Let me see," he said, reaching into the velvet sack he had brought with him, "who is going to be first?"

At the chorus of "Me!" that rang through the room, Armando let out a deep rumbling laugh worthy of the Babbo himself.

Rosa's heart warmed at the sight. She had known from the very beginning that playing Santa would be a balm for Armando's grief, but it never ceased to amaze her how good he was at the job. He made sure every child got special one-on-one time with Babbo, he treated them as miniature adults, going along with the pretense for the children's sake. He was going to make a wonderful father.

When he had children with Mona. Beautiful, royal children. A wave of envy, fierce and cold, sent her spirits plummeting.

Max, who she didn't realize had disappeared, returned carrying a pair of paper coffee cups. "All this time I've been thinking Babbo Natale was some old-world European tradition and it turns out he's a more athletic version of Santa Claus," he said, tilting his head to where Armando was teasing a young girl with a stuffed rabbit. "I feel cheated."

"If it makes you feel better, there are Corinthians who embrace Befana."

"What's that?"

"An Italian witch who arrives on Epiphany."

The American's lips turned downward. "A witch on Christmas?"

"More like a crone. She brings treats."

"In that case, yes, I do feel better." He handed her one of the paper cups. "Turns out marrying the princess comes with some benefits. I mentioned wanting an espresso and the caterer made me two. You look like you could use a cup."

"Thank you." Caffeine sounded like just what she needed to perk her sagging mood. "Speaking of Arianna, where is she?"

"Putting up her feet in the back room," he replied. "Sitting on the piano stool for so long was hard on her back."

"She should have said something."

"Are you kidding? You know what Arianna's like when it comes to pianos. She was having way too much fun." From the center of the room, a child let out a high-pitched squeal. "Sounds like they're having fun, too," he noted.

"Who? The children or Prince Armando?"

"Both. I think this is the first time I've actually seen Arianna's brother smile. Granted, I've only known him about a week, so I might be misjudging…"

"No, you're not," Rosa replied, thinking of the media's nickname. "Prince Armando isn't known for his jovial side in public. This is definitely one of the few events where he truly lets himself relax and enjoy the moment."

"Hard not to enjoy yourself when you're around children," she added, as out on the floor Armando scooped up another toddler. "Although some people can't shake their mean streaks no matter what. If they could, we wouldn't need a place like Christina's Home." Wives wouldn't be made to feel like second-class citizens simply because they weren't perfect or, heaven forbid, carried a few extra pounds.

"Tell me about it," Max said. The bitterness in his voice surprised her. "Only thing that made my old man happy was a bottle. Or smacking my mom."

Rosa winced. "Some people need to mistreat their loved ones to feel better about themselves."

"That sounds like personal knowledge."

"A little."

He paused to look at her over his cup. "Your father was an A-hole, too? Pardon the language."

"No, my ex-husband." Normally, she avoided talking about Fredo, especially here at the shelter where there were women who had suffered far worse than she, but it was hard to brush off a kindred spirit. "And the word you used is a very apt description."

"I'm sorry."

Rosa stared at her untouched espresso, grateful he didn't press for more. But then, one of things about a kindred spirit was they didn't want to share either, so not asking worked to their benefit. "Me, too," she replied. "But at least when I finally worked up the courage to leave, I had people to turn to. I'm not sure what I would have done otherwise." Most likely, she would be with Fredo still, fifty pounds heavier and with her self-esteem completely eroded.

"So Christina's Home is more than a memorial to your sister then," Max said.

"My sister would have been the first person to say we need places like Christina's Home," she replied. She also would have been horrified to learn about the truth of Rosa's marriage. "But yes. If someone like me, with connections to the king, of all people, had trouble working up the courage to leave, I can't imagine what it is like for a woman who has no one."

Max's tight smile said he knew but wasn't going to talk about it. "At least you left eventually. More power to you."

Much to Rosa's relief, he tossed his crumpled paper cup into a nearby trash bin, indicating the conversation was over. "I better go check on Arianna and make sure she's truly resting. She's only just over the morning sickness stuff, and I don't want her pushing herself more than she needs to."

"If she's anything like her brother, she will," Rosa replied. "When the Santoros make a commitment, they do so one hundred and ten percent. It's ingrained in their DNA."

"No kidding. I almost lost Arianna because of it," Max replied. "Wish me luck getting her to put her feet up."

"Good luck," She waited until he'd moved away before letting her smile fade. Talking about Fredo had taken the edge off her holiday cheer.

"Is it true?" a familiar voice asked.

Armando stood behind her, still in costume. His eyes were like bright blue glass amid all his fake white hair. "What you told Max about Fredo, is it true?"

Dammit. How much had he heard? Rosa wanted to look anywhere but at him and those eyes filled with questions and…and pity. Exactly what she didn't want to see. God, looking her reflection in the eye was hard enough. How was she supposed to look at him every day if he saw her as some kind of…of…victim?

"I'm going to get some more cake," she announced. She didn't want to talk about Fredo right now, and cake never asked questions.

"Rosa, wait." He chased after her, catching her hand just as she got to the serving table.

"Armando," she whispered harshly, "the children."

Armando looked around, saw several of the youngest ones watching their interaction, and released her hand. "Why didn't you tell me?" he asked.

"Because…" She didn't finish. The anguish in her eyes answered for her, and it nearly kicked the legs out from under him. "It's in the past. What does it matter now?"

It mattered to him. If he had known, he might have done something. Stopped it somehow.

All those nights discussing the shelter… He'd thought Rosa's passion lay in memorializing her sister, but he'd been wrong. While he had been waxing sympathetic about the women they were helping, Rosa never said a word. How long had she suffered? Why hadn't he or Christina noticed? Were they so caught up in their own worlds they missed the signs? Or had Rosa been skilled at hiding them? His stomach ached for wondering. The strength it must have taken for her to walk away, the courage.

He took a good long look at the woman he'd been calling his right hand these last three years. She looked the same as always, and yet it was as though he was seeing her for the first time. What else didn't he know about her?

Suddenly he wanted to be free of the party so the two of them could talk. He had so many questions. Before he realized, he was taking her hand again. The anguish flashed in her eyes again. "Armando…" she pleaded.

Fine. He wouldn't push her right now. That didn't mean the conversation was over. He had too many questions—was too angry and ashamed of himself—to let the subject drop. "Just tell me one thing," he asked. "Did Christina know?"

She shook her head. "No."

In a weird way, he found himself relieved. He wasn't sure how he would feel if he'd discovered Christina had known, but apparently Rosa had suffered in silence. If only he'd known…

Someone tugged on his hem of his jacket. "Babbo, Babbo, Babbo!"

Damn this costume. Biting back a sigh, he instead turned to see what his visitor found so urgent.

A pair of blond pigtails and giant brown eyes looked up at him. Armando recognized the girl from earlier, a five-year-old named Daniela who had gotten a circus play set. In fact, she held one of the set's plastic elephants in her hand. Quickly he cleared his voice. Wasn't the child's fault she'd interrupted an important moment. "Ho, ho, ho, Daniela. You're not trying to get another early present out of me, are you?" he asked, hoping his voice sounded lighthearted.

The little girl shook her head. "You're standing under the mistletoe."

What? He looked up and saw the familiar sprig of white berries dangling from a ceiling panel. "And you want a kiss from Babbo, is that it?"

Again, Daniela shook her head. "You have to kiss her," she said pointing behind him. Slowly, he turned to Rosa, whose hand he still held. Which was the only reason she was still standing there, if the look on her face was any indication.

His eyes dropped to her lips, causing his pulse to skip. He hadn't kissed a woman since Christina's death.

Meanwhile, some of the older children who had been standing near the refreshment table figured out what was happening and began chanting in a singsong chorus, "Babbo's under the mistletoe. Babbo's under the mistletoe." The little devils. The lot of them were old enough to know his true identity, too. Probably thought it would be funny to make the prince kiss someone. He looked back at Daniela.

"Aren't I supposed to kiss the person who caught me under the mistletoe?" he asked. A quick peck on the little girl's cheek to quiet everyone.

"No. It has to be her. She was the one standing with you."

"Kiss her. Kiss her," the other children started chanting. Didn't they have parents to teach them how to behave?

"Babbo has to leave to go back to his workshop," Rosa said. In the short time since he'd turned toward her, her expression had transformed from wanting to flee to sheer terror. Armando's ego winced. Surely the idea of kissing him couldn't be that terrible?

"Daniela is right, signora," he said. "Tradition is tradition. You wouldn't want to break tradition, would you?"

"I—I suppose not." Her gaze dropped to her feet. She had very long lashes, he realized. Reminded him of tiny black fans.

"Good." It was only one small kiss. The two of them could argue about its awkwardness tomorrow morning.

Still holding her hand, he slipped his other arm around her waist and pulled her close. It was, he realized, the first time he'd ever put his arms around her, and he discovered her body was as pleasantly soft and curvy as it looked. The swell of her behind rested just beneath his splayed fingers, and it seemed to dare him to slip his hand lower. Instead, he focused on her lips, which were apparently as dry as his mouth had suddenly become, because she was running her tongue across the lower one. Her lips looked pleasantly soft and full, too.

"Kiss her. Kiss her," the children chanted.

He dipped his head.

The kiss lasted five seconds. When he stepped away, Rosa's cheeks were bright pink, and he...

His lips were tingling.

He didn't know what to say. "I—"

"Gelato," Rosa cut in. "I—I mean, we need to check the gelato." She turned and hurried toward the kitchen.

"Rosa, wait," he called after her, but she disappeared behind closed doors without turning around. Apparently the moment hadn't erased her desire to flee their discussion.

"Are you all right, Babbo?" Daniela asked. The little girl's eyes were wide with concern.

"That's a good question, Daniela." Looking back to the kitchen door, Armando ran his tongue across his lip, which tasted faintly of espresso. Was he?

CHAPTER FOUR

By TIMING HER comings and goings around Armando's schedule, Rosa was able to avoid the man for much of the next week. She was being a coward, yes, but she needed the space considering the way she'd reacted to Armando's kiss.

Hardly a kiss. A peck under the mistletoe. Yet here she was, reliving every detail from the way his lips tasted—like breath mints— to the sensation of his artificial beard against her skin. He was right—it scratched.

She was running her finger across her lips again. *Stop it, stop it, stop it.* Balling her fingers, she tried hammering her fist against the chair arm in time with her silent chant, only the rhythm was too similar to *Kiss her, kiss her, kiss her.* Before she could help herself, the chants had switched.

Apparently her increased awareness wasn't going away any time soon.

It was all so awkward and weird, this sudden realization that Armando was a man. She could only assume his getting married caused her subconscious to wake up as far as dating was concerned. Why else would her chest be filled with a hollow, jealous ache whenever she thought about it? She wanted what Armando would have. Or so she was telling herself. She didn't want to contemplate the other reason for her reactions.

As for Armando...the kiss obviously hadn't fazed him. He'd left a note the other morning saying that Mona would be attending the Christina's Home concert on Friday night. Escorting the woman to his late wife's memorial concert would certainly let Corinthia know he was ready to move on.

Hammering her fist on the chair arm again, she sat back and took another look at the morning's paper. In the upper left-hand corner ran Mona's photo with a headline that read Our New Princess? A small story on the inside page reported on Armando's growing closeness with the Yelgierian royal family as of late, and implied there would be a marriage announcement soon.

"We missed you last evening." Princess Arianna strolled into the office without notice, knocking not being a royal requirement. She was dressed casually—for her, anyway—in a simple black skirt and flowing pink silk blouse. In deference to her pregnancy, the hem hung untucked. "At the tree lighting," she added. "You didn't attend."

The tree lighting, when King Carlos lit the tree in the palace's grand archway, marked the official start of Corinthia's holiday season. Until last night, Rosa had attended almost every one. Next to the shelter festival, it was one of her favorite Christmas traditions.

"I'm sorry," she said. "I simply had too much work to do to get away."

"Funny, Armando didn't mention you were working. In fact, he didn't seem to know where you were."

But he hadn't been looking for her, either. "I worked at home," she replied. "Armando… that is, he didn't know I was behind."

"Is that so?" Rosa tried not to react when

the princess looked down at her pristinely organized desk. People with neat desks could be busy, too.

"Maybe he should get you some help. It's not fair that you have so much work that you have to miss a Corinthian tradition."

"That's not necessary, Your Highness. I'm caught up now." That was all she needed, to look like she couldn't handle her workload.

"Glad to hear it," Arianna replied, "because I would kill Armando if you were too busy to celebrate with us next week. Which reminds me, you are coming to the dinner, are you not?"

"I— Are you sure you want me there?" The dinner was a private affair for family and dignitaries the night before the ceremony.

"Of course I do," Arianna replied. "You're family, aren't you?"

"Technically, no."

"Close enough. You're an important part of Armando's life, and therefore you're important to all of us."

"How can I say no after that?" Rosa replied, surprised to feel a lump in her throat. It had been a long time since someone had said she was anything other than a stupid waste of time. And while the idea of spending an evening watching Armando and Mona get acquainted left a sour taste in her mouth, the princess was smiling such a sweet, sincere smile, Rosa didn't have the heart to decline.

Besides, she would have to face Armando—and Mona—eventually. Maybe seeing them together would kill the weird feelings she was having.

Meanwhile, Arianna's smile grew broader upon Rosa's acceptance. "I'm so glad. Max's best friend from New York is coming, too, and I can't wait for the two of you to meet. Not for romantic reasons," she added when Rosa started to say something. "I just think he needs a dinner partner who will keep him on his toes."

"Oh. Thank you, I guess." She couldn't imagine keeping anyone other than Armando on his toes, but if Arianna thought so, she would try.

"It's a compliment, I assure you." Perching on the edge of Rosa's desk, Arianna turned the newspaper around. "Future princess, huh? Wonder where they came up with that idea?"

"I read the article. It's mostly speculation."

Arianna arched her brow. "I'm going to blame your naïveté on not having enough coffee. Armando hasn't dated since Christina passed away, and out of the blue the press start speculating on the exact woman he plans to marry? Impossible. Someone whispered in a reporter's ear. The only question is who is doing the whispering—Armando or King Omar. My guess is on Armando."

Rosa didn't understand. Princess Arianna's explanation about a leak made perfect sense, but she would think King Omar the more likely source, not her brother. "Why would His Highness leak information about his private life?"

"Because I know how my big brother's mind works. I'm starting to show. It's obvious to anyone who can add that I've been pregnant longer than I've known Max." A soft smile curled her lips as her hand patted her abdomen. She glanced back at the photograph. "This is Armando's way of diverting attention away from my growing bump."

Made sense. After all, he'd arranged a marriage to prevent scandal. Why not arrange for a little well-timed tabloid gossip, too? "He's trying to be a good king," she said.

"That's Armando. Corinthia and family first."

Responsible for every light in every window. "He takes fulfilling his duty very seriously," she replied.

"Always has," Arianna said. "Although he's gotten worse the last couple years. Sometimes I think he's decided that if he can't be happy anymore, he'll make sure everyone else in Corinthia is."

Rosa's heart twisted at the thought. She didn't know what bothered her more, Armando falling for his wife or him going through the motions for the rest of his life.

"Speaking of my brother, what do you think?"

It took a moment for Rosa to realize the princess was talking about Mona herself. Took a lot of discipline, but she managed to swallow the sour taste in her mouth before replying. "I wouldn't know, Your Highness."

"Please," the princess replied. She added an eye roll for good measure. "Don't go into acting, Rosa. You're terrible."

"But I really wouldn't know," Rosa replied honestly. "I haven't met her. She's very beautiful, though. And her father certainly speaks highly of her."

"Fathers usually do," Arianna replied. "According to mine, I am the purest creature to ever walk the earth." Her grin was nothing short of cheeky as she pointed to her midsection. "I think I'll wait until I've met the woman to see if she lives up to her advance praise. Armando says she's attending the concert tonight?"

"Yes. She is supposed to arrive late this afternoon." Rosa had been trying to figure out an excuse to avoid her arrival all week.

"You don't look happy about the idea."

"Excuse me?" So much for keeping her thoughts private. She really was a terrible actress.

"No worries," Arianna replied. "I understand. This is a concert for your sister, and here's Armando infringing upon her memory by introducing his future wife."

"No, that's not the reason." Everyone was so quick to blame her loyalty to Christina. Armando thought the same thing regarding the shelter party. The simple, shameful truth, however, had nothing to do with Christina.

"What is the reason then?"

Rosa opened, then shut her mouth. What did she say? She couldn't very well tell Armando's sister the truth—that she was dreading a night of simultaneous jealousy and embarrassment.

Fortunately the telephone saved her. When she heard the voice on the other end, her eyes widened.

"That was King Omar's secretary," she said when she hung up. "Apparently his daughter hasn't completely recovered from the flu and is feeling too ill to fly."

"Meaning she's not coming tonight?"

"I'm afraid not." Rosa's stomach took a happy little bounce at the news, even though she knew it shouldn't.

From Arianna's expression, she didn't do a good job of hiding her reaction, either. "Armando will be disappointed," she noted.

Immediately Rosa was ashamed of herself.

"Yes," she said, "I imagine he will be." He no doubt meant for this appearance to be Mona's introduction to the Corinthian people.

"Where is my dear brother, anyway?" Arianna asked. "I came by because I wanted to talk to him about a rumored cut to the arts endowment budget."

"According to the note he left on my desk, he is at the swimming pool doing laps."

"Really? Max is swimming laps right now as well." With surprising spryness for a pregnant woman, the princess hopped off the desk. "I was planning to go visit him after I spoke to Armando. Why don't the two of us go together and you can tell Armando about Mona's cancellation?"

See Armando. At the pool. That happy little bounce turned into a shiver as she pictured a muscular and wet Armando emerging from the water like a men's fragrance advertisement come to life. "I thought I would send him a text…" she started.

"Don't be silly. I don't feel like waiting for him to check his messages before talking to him about it. Come down with me, and we will tell him in person."

This was the downside of working for royalty. It was impossible to refuse when they decided a plan of action. Suppressing a sigh, Rosa pushed to her feet. "After you, Your Highness."

Maybe she'd get lucky, and Armando would stay in the water while they talked.

The pool was an Olympic-size addition built in what had been an unused greenhouse on the edge of the palace gardens in the mid–twentieth century. When his children were younger, King Carlos had the aging facility refurbished, transforming what had been a bland indoor pool into a paradise filled with flowers and soothing flowing water. The bamboo and hibiscus served as more than decoration—they created a foliage privacy wall so that the royal family could relax in peace. For as long as Rosa had known Armando, the room had been one of his favorite places. Since moving into the palace, Max, had taken to visiting the pool as well.

A block of hot humid air hit Rosa when she opened the door to the building. It'd been a while since she'd visited Armando in his sanctuary, and so she had forgotten how much of a contrast there was between here and the garden path that connected the two buildings, especially during the winter. She could feel her shirt starting to stick against her skin in the dampness, destroying every bit of flowing camouflage. Wasn't worth pulling the garment free, either, since it would only cling right back.

A shout called her attention toward the pool where Armando and Max were splashing their way from one end to the other.

"Looks like they are racing," Rosa remarked.

"Of course they are. They're men," Princess Arianna replied. She did peel her shirt away from her skin. "This is the first time I've ever watched Max swim. I didn't know he was such a good swimmer."

He was definitely the faster of the two—his pale body was a good length ahead—but Armando had better style. His bronze shoulders rose up and down in the water, like a well-tuned piston. Rosa envied how he could be graceful both on land and in the water.

Unsurprisingly, Max reached the wall

first. When he realized Arianna and Rosa were standing there, he pulled himself out of the water.

"Well, isn't this a pleasant surprise?" he said, leaning forward to give Arianna a kiss. From the way he twisted his body, he was doing everything he could not to let his wet body come in contact with hers.

Rosa couldn't help but look him up and down. The man was definitely as well built as his movie-star looks implied. Princess Arianna was a lucky woman.

Armando's voice sounded behind her. "Next time, we do more. We'll see if you're so fast when you have to make a turn, eh? Can someone hand me a towel?"

Someone being her, of course. Rosa should have known he wouldn't stay in the water. There was a large white one draped over the back of a nearby chair. Steeling herself for what she was about to see, Rosa grabbed it and turned around.

Oh, my.

Forget fragrance ad come to life. Try sea god.

Anyone who met the man could tell Armando was well built simply from the way his clothes draped his body. What the clothes didn't show was how virile he was. He made Max Brown look like a young boy. Awareness spread from her core as she took in the muscular, wet body, its contours glistening under the lights. Droplets clung to his chest hair, like tiny crystal ornaments. Wordlessly, she watched as he wiped them away with the towel, her breath catching a little on each stroke across his skin.

If she couldn't stop thinking about a peck on the lips…

"Rosa?"

She jerked her attention back to his face to find him looking at her with unusual intensity. "Is everything all right?" he asked. "You looked flushed."

Because you're beautiful. "It's the heat," she replied. "It's like a sauna in here."

"Well, the room was designed for people in bathing suits." He wrapped the towel around his waist, and Rosa let out a breath. Never did she think wearing a towel would be modest. "I said I was surprised to see you. You've been avoiding me."

He'd noticed? Of course he had. She hadn't exactly been subtle about staying away. "No, I haven't," she lied anyway. "There is a lot going on, is all. I have been very busy coordinating the various year-end events."

"Right. Coordinating. I understand," he said in a voice that said he didn't believe her in the slightest. "Why are you here now, then? Did something happen?"

His eyes had not just dropped to her lips and back. He was a man about to marry an amazing beauty. The last thing he would waste time on was their mistletoe kiss, unless he was remembering her foolish bolt through the kitchen door.

"I—" Rosa began. This would have been so much easier if Arianna had let her send a text. Thanks to his half-dressed state, the moment felt far more intimate than it was. What was more, the princess wasn't even talking to Armando. She and Max had taken themselves to one of the many lounge chairs, leaving her and Armando alone.

"King Omar's office called. Mona is still feeling ill and won't be able to attend the concert tonight."

"Oh."

That was an…odd reaction. Detached and almost relieved sounding. Surely that couldn't be the case. "I thought I should let you know as soon as possible in case this affects your plans for the evening."

"You could have texted."

"Arianna wanted me to tell you in person."

"Oh." That answer did come with a reaction. A conspiratorial smile that said he understood exactly what had happened. They usually shared dozens of such smiles during the course of a normal week. Seeing this one made her feel all melty inside. She'd missed his company, dammit.

"Anyway…" She cleared her throat. "If you would like to cancel…"

"Cancel? Why on earth would I cancel?"

"I only thought that with Mona not attending…" Seeing his frown, she left her answer hanging. "Never mind."

"Never mind is right. I can't believe you even suggested I wouldn't attend." He headed toward a bench by one of the bamboo trees where a robe and additional towels lay. As he brushed past her, his bare shoulder made contact with hers, and Rosa's insides turned to jitters at the feeling of dampness through her blouse. It was as close to skin against skin as she'd felt in a long time.

"You're right," she replied, rubbing the goose bumps from her arms. "I don't know what I was thinking. This morning's newspaper article speculating on your marriage must have skewed my reasoning."

He was flipping a towel around his neck when she asked. Gripping both ends, he cocked his head. "What does that mean?"

"It means, I know it was to be an important public appearance for the two of you." The first step in establishing the seriousness of their relationship."

An odd look crossed his features. "Right. I forgot about the gossip column. It would have been nice to have Mona make an appearance, but seeing as how the marriage is all but a fait accompli, it's not completely necessary.

"Besides," he added as he reached for his robe, "it's not as if the people aren't used to seeing me attend events alone.

"You're still attending, right?" he asked, shrugging into the robe.

"Of course. It's my sister's memorial concert. I wouldn't miss it for the world." Not even Mona's presence would have stopped her. "I can't believe you asked."

"What are you talking about? You asked me the same question two minutes ago. And, considering I haven't seen you all week, I didn't want to assume."

There was a bite to his comment that took her aback. She thought they had addressed this. "I told you, I have had a lot to take care of this week."

"Coordinating. So you said." He tugged on his terry-cloth belt before looking her in the eye. Rosa tried not to squirm, but the intensity of his stare was too unnerving. He was trying to see inside her again. "Look, I know why you have been avoiding me," he said.

"You do?" Heaven help her, could they go back to talking about Mona? Please? Not only was her embarrassing reaction to their mistletoe kiss the last thing she wanted to talk about, this was the last place where she wanted to not talk about it—in a steamy pool house with him wearing nothing but a bathrobe.

"I owe you an apology."

"You do?" she repeated. For what?

"It was…rude…of me to confront you the way I did. Regarding Fredo. I put you on the spot, and I shouldn't have."

"I see." She had forgotten their argument about Fredo, her mind focused on their kiss. Apparently, circumstances were the other way around for Armando. He wasn't thinking about the kiss at all. Which was a good thing, right? Meant she didn't have to avoid him anymore.

There was no reason for her insides to feel deflated. "Th-thank you," she replied. "I appreciate that."

On the other side of the pool, Arianna and Max lay side by side in one of the lounge chairs. Max had slipped on his bathrobe, and the two of them looked to be in deep conversation. Whatever problem Arianna had with the budget seemed to have taken a backseat to her fiancé. They looked so happy and engrossed with each other. Maybe it was talking about Fredo, but looking at them left Rosa aching with envy. What she wouldn't give for a man who listened to what she had to say with interest instead of patronizing her or putting her down. Someone who respected her and didn't continually remind her of her many, many flaws. *You're fat. You sound like an idiot.*

A girl could dream, couldn't she? Even if the odds of a woman like her finding someone like Max Brown were slim to none. Heck, the only person she knew who fit her bill was... Max.

She turned back in time to discover Armando was studying her again. Only this time, instead of feeling like he was looking inside her, she broke out in a tingling, achy sensation that cut through her stomach to deep below her waist.

"Get dressed," she said abruptly. "I mean, you need to get dressed and I...I should get back to the office. I'll see you when you return."

Spinning on her toe of her shoe, she turned and headed toward the pool house door. Arianna was right about her acting skills. At least this time, her excuse sounded better than having to double-check gelato quantities.

"Rosa, wait."

* * *

Armando chuckled when Rosa turned around. She looked like an animal trapped in the headlights of an automobile. Wide-eyed and hesitant. And damn if he didn't find it appealing.

"Are you bringing a guest to the concert?" he asked.

He could tell she didn't know what to make of his question. "You mean, do I have a date?"

"Exactly. I was curious if, after our conversation the other day, you weren't inspired to…improve…your social life."

Was that a blush creeping into her cheeks or simply a flush from the warm air? "You're curious about a lot of things lately."

About her, he was. It disturbed him to realize he didn't know her as well as he thought. Like the proverbial onion, there were layers he'd yet to peel back, and dammit if he didn't want to see what lay beneath. "Are you?" he asked.

"No," she replied after a pause. "I haven't had the opportunity to…improve…anything. I've been busy."

"Why don't we sit together, then?"

Rosa nearly choked. "Together? As in sit with you in the front row of the royal box?"

"Why not? Now that Mona isn't attending, the seat next to me will be empty."

"Yes, but I always sit behind you at royal events."

A rule of her own making. Armando couldn't care less about seating arrangements. In fact, it sometimes aggravated him the way Rosa would stick herself in the background, as though she were afraid to take up space. "Well, tonight I'd like you to sit in the front row with me."

"I—"

"As you said, this concert is as important to you as it is me. Tonight will be the last concert I will host before I get married. This is our opportunity to pay homage to Christina together one last time."

A shadow darkened her features. Using Christina was a low blow, but her sister's memory was the one thing Rosa couldn't resist. "I suppose," she said in a soft voice.

"Good, it's settled. We'll attend together. I will pick you up at your apartment at seven."

"Fine. Seven o'clock," she replied. "Is there anything else?"

Yes, she could try to sound a little excited. "Feel free to take the afternoon off. I know how you women like to primp for these things."

"Thank you," she replied. Armando wondered if she was grateful for the extra preparation time or the chance to avoid him a little longer. Just because she seemed to accept his apology didn't mean she wasn't still upset with him, as her reluctance to attend the concert together showed.

He watched as she turned and continued to the door. Damn, but he hated those long blazers of hers. This one was charcoal gray and went to the hem of her skirt. If there was one thing he'd noticed over the years it was that Rosa had an unparalleled walk, as good as any of the runway models in Milan. Whenever she moved, she led with her pelvis, causing her hips to swivel from side to side. And, because unlike a runway model, she carried some actual meat on her bones, her bottom half undulated with a fluidity that was amazingly sensual. Reminded him of wine swirling in a glass.

Except when she wore those blasted blazers. If she tried to wear one tonight, he would burn it.

"Was that Rosa leaving?" Arianna asked when the door clicked shut.

"I gave her the afternoon off," he replied. "She's attending the concert with me—that is, we're going to cohost the event." The other way made it sound like a date, which this wasn't. No matter how his body had reacted when she said yes.

"What a nice idea," his sister said.

"I thought we should since Mona is unable to come." And it would be their last opportunity.

Did his relief upon hearing Mona had canceled make him a horrible person? One would think he would want to spend time with his prospective bride. Wasn't that why he'd invited her to the concert in the first place? So they could get to know each other?

And then he could start fantasizing about her rather than about the kiss he'd shared with Rosa.

He shoved that last thought to the back of his mind where it belonged. He was not fantasizing about Rosa. Not really. She was his sister-in-law, for crying out loud. His sex drive had reawakened, that was all. A man could only live as a monk for so long, and Rosa happened to be the woman who was there when his inner male returned.

As for tonight, it was only fitting they co-host the event. To honor Christina.

And if he wanted to make sure she had a proper time? Well, that was simply because she deserved an enjoyable evening and had nothing to do with wanting to make her feel special.

Nothing at all.

CHAPTER FIVE

WHAT HAD SHE been thinking? Rosa smoothed
her hands along her hips. When she tried it
on, the saleswoman flattered her to Rome
and back with a pitch about how this dress's
straight cut accentuated her figure rather
than making her look large and hippy. Flush
from the ego boost, Rosa had let herself be
talked into going against her normal style.
It wasn't just the silhouette that was out of
character; it was the bright red color and
slightly bare shoulders, too. *Live a little*,
she'd thought at the time. *No one's going to
care what you wear.*

That was before she knew she would be
sitting in the front row.

Next to Armando.

As his date.

Not a date. Calling tonight a date made

the evening sound like it was something special rather than two friends attending an event together. Which the two of them had done dozens of times before. The only thing different about tonight was the seating arrangement.

And the fact he was picking her up.

And that the concert would be broadcast across all of Corinthia. With her seated by Armando's side, which would make her look like his date.

Had he known that when he asked her?

Her palms started to sweat. Moving to rub them on her skirt, she caught herself in time.

Squaring her shoulders, she turned left, then right, looking for any unshapely bumps or bulges. The saleswoman had been right about one thing—the dress certainly emphasized her shape. Daily walking had made her legs firm and toned, while good old control-top undergarments had firmed up the rest. She looked, dare she say it, not that bad. If only the dress weren't bright. So attention seeking.

What makes you think anyone is going to be looking at you?

Three years and Fredo's voice was as loud as ever in her head, taking her confidence and crushing it into bits.

You're a cow. You're an embarrassment.

The last thing she wanted was to embarrass Armando.

Maybe she had time to change. The black dress from last Christmas, he had liked that one, hadn't he? Or the navy blue one she wore two years ago with the sequined bodice. Could she still fit into it?

She never stressed like this over dresses before.

Then again, she'd never been Armando's date before. Not a date, she quickly amended.

Just then her living room clock chimed seven. Barely had the last clang sounded when the doorbell rang. Rosa jumped. What the— Three years of having to hustle him out the door, and the one night he had to get ready without her, he was on time?

She opened the door to find him with one shoulder propped against the door frame. Naturally, he looked amazing, the stiff white collar gleaming against his darker skin. In a flash, Rosa's mind peeled off the clothing to picture the man she saw swimming this morning. All six feet three inches of carved muscle.

"Hi." The greeting came out a breathy whisper, far too intimate sounding for the circumstances. She cringed inwardly.

Armando eyes widened. "You look…"

She knew it. The dress was too bright.

"Gorgeous," he finished. "I mean it, that dress is…"

"Thank you. The woman at the boutique talked me into trying something different."

"Good for her. You should wear red more often. The color suits you."

Rosa hoped so, because now her cheeks were the same color as her dress, a combination of modesty and embarrassment over her reaction. This wasn't the first time Armando had ever paid her a compliment, yet awareness ghosted across her skin like it was. Made her feel more feminine and beautiful than she had in years. "You look nice, too," she told him, looking up through her lashes. "Very…regal."

"Damn. I was going for dashing."

Mission definitely accomplished. Almost. "One little thing," she said. His tie was crooked. "You never can get your tie proper," she said, reaching up.

"That's because you weren't there to help me," he replied, lifting his chin. "Arianna had to tie it for me."

"Well, that explains why it's better than usual."

Rosa felt his warm breath on the top of her head as she adjusted the tie. Despite having done this dozens of times, she'd never noticed the distinctness of his aftershave until now. Reminded her of a wood after summer rain, earthy and cool. The kind of scent that made a person want to run barefoot through the moss.

Or comb their fingers through their hair.

"There." Smoothing his collar, she stepped back before her thoughts could embarrass her again. "Much better."

He gave her a smile. "Whatever would I do without you?"

"Spend eternity with a crooked tie, for one thing." Once again, her body reacted as though he weren't making a comment he'd made before. This was ridiculous. Tonight was really no different from any other night. Why, then, was she acting as though it was? Surely she wasn't so desperate for male validation that her subconscious needed to assign deeper meaning to everything Armando said and did. "I just need to get my wrap and I'll be ready to go."

"You're not…"

"What?" She'd not gotten more than a few feet before he spoke. Turning around, she caught the hint of a blush crawling down his cheekbones.

"You're not going to put on some jacket and wear it all night, are you?"

"No. Just a velvet wrap for when we're outside. Why?"

"No reason," he replied quickly. "It's… well, I'm not as big a fan of jackets as you are."

"I wouldn't be either, if I had your rock-hard abdomen." Rosa squeezed her eyes shut. Please say she didn't speak those words aloud.

Armando chuckled as he sauntered toward her. "You were looking at my abdomen, were you?"

"Not on purpose. It's difficult to ignore a man's torso when he's standing in a bathing suit."

"I see. Well, I'm glad you found my torso to your satisfaction."

"That's not what I meant."

"Oh?" He reached around her to lift her wrap from where it lay draped on the back of her chair. "What did you mean, then?"

"Simply that your midsection doesn't need camouflaging."

"Neither does yours," he replied, laying the velvet across her shoulders. "You worry too much about your weight. Curves are to be celebrated. There's a reason Botticelli didn't paint stick figures, you know," he added, low in her ear.

Rosa's knees nearly buckled at the way his breath tickled her skin. "I'll try to remember that."

"Please do. There's nothing worse than listening to a beautiful woman denigrate herself."

"Nothing?" Rosa asked, trying to react to the word *beautiful*. He'd handed her more compliments in the past five minutes than she'd had in the last decade.

His returning smile was devastating. "Well, maybe not as bad as reviewing the revised energy regulations or listening to Arianna complain about the arts endowment, but definitely bad." He held out an arm. "Shall we?"

No matter how many times Rosa told herself that technically this evening was no different than any other, Armando and the evening kept proving her wrong. To begin with, there was a lot of difference between sitting in the rear of the royal box and sitting with the crown prince. In the past she would take her seat several minutes before the performance and patiently wait along with everyone else for Armando to take his seat. Tonight, she was the one hanging back while the audience assembled, the one receiving the applause as she entered the box at the Royal Opera House. Really it was Armando receiving the applause, but standing by his side, she couldn't help but feel special, too.

Armando himself was contributing to the feeling as well. She couldn't put her finger on how, but there was something about his behavior tonight. He was solicitous, charming. Flirtatious, even, peppering his conversation with subtle touches and low, lilting commentary. The skin behind her ear still tingled from their conversation in her apartment. *Curves are to be celebrated.*

She squeezed her knees together.

"Everything all right?" Armando asked, mistaking her shifting as discomfort.

"Just sitting up straight," she replied. "I don't want to get caught on camera slouching."

"Fortunately, most of the time they stay focused on the orchestra, or so I've been told. I was afraid you might not be having a good time."

"Why would you think that?" she asked, doing her best not to frown as she turned toward him.

"I don't know, perhaps because you've been avoiding me all week. I wasn't sure if you were still angry with me."

"I was never angry with you. I had a lot to do, is all."

"Then you weren't annoyed that I asked about Fredo?"

He was kidding, right? What was it that drove him to introduce awkward conversations at the most inopportune times?

"I know," he added when she opened her mouth, "you don't want to talk about him right now."

No, she did not, but now that the door was open, she figured she should at least give him a quick explanation. "Nothing personal. In my experience, anything to do with Fredo will only spoil a good time." As far as she was concerned, her ex was an ugly cloud she'd rather forget.

She started as a hand settled atop her forearm. Looking up, she noticed Armando wore a pleased expression. "Does that mean you're having a good time?"

"Very."

"Good." His hand squeezed her arm and then remained. "I'm glad. You deserve the best evening possible," he added in a low voice. His whispered breath caressed her jaw, reminding her of gentle fingertips. Thankfully, the house lights had started to dim, hiding how her skin flushed from the inside out.

Onstage, the conductor emerged from behind a curtain, drawing another round of applause. After bowing to Armando, the man stepped on his dais and tapped his baton. Like a well-trained army, the musicians raised their instruments. A moment later, the room filled with the delicate hum of violins.

"Don't tell my family," Armando whispered in her ear. Between the dark and the hand on her arm, the innocent comment sent a trail of goose bumps down her spine. "But I do not like classical music."

"Since when?" Considering the way his sister and late mother had revered music, the confession wasn't just shocking, it was almost treasonous.

"Since ever," he replied. "Why do you think Arianna is the only one who still plays the piano? As soon as I could, I stopped lessons and haven't touched a keyboard since."

"I didn't realize." Both that he disliked classical music and that he played piano. Keeping her eyes forward, she leaned her shoulder closer to his. There was something naughty about whispering together in the dark. "How long did you have to take lessons?"

"Twelve very long years."

That long? "Why didn't you stop sooner?"

"Because it was expected I would become a master."

Expected. Sadly his answer didn't surprise her. So much of what he did stemmed from expectations or tradition. Even this concert, in a way. Made her wonder how long it had been since he did anything purely for fun.

She settled back against her seat as the music crescendoed over them. "Does this mean I'll need to poke you in the ribs to keep you from nodding off?" she whispered.

"Don't be silly. I never fall asleep."

"Never?"

"Okay, not since I was twelve. I have a secret trick."

"What's that?" she asked.

Behind them, Vittorio Mastella, the head of security, gave a sharp cough, and Rosa bit her lip. Because it was the crown prince doing the whispering, no one was going to say anything directly, but apparently the security chief had no problem delivering a subtle hint. Armando smiled and winked. "I'll tell you after the concert," he whispered.

They spent the rest of the concert in silence. Unlike Armando, Rosa did enjoy classical music, although purely as an amateur. She hadn't had many opportunities to enjoy it when she was married, since Fredo would only attend a concert if there was business involved. The few times they did attend, however, were some of the best memories of her marriage. She would sit in the dark and let the music send her to a world far away, to a place where she was beautiful and happy. Like the Rosa she used to be.

As the music washed over her tonight, she realized she already felt beautiful and happy. Whether it was the dress or Armando's appreciative words or the two combined, she was content with herself for the first time in a long time. More than content—it was as though she'd woken up from a long sleep and remembered she was a woman. Her body was suddenly aware of even the lightest of touches. Armando shifted in his seat, and the brush of his pant leg against her ankle left her insides aching. It did not help that he shifted in his seat a lot. Nor the fact that his hand lingered on her forearm till midway through the concert, his long fingers absently tapping a melody against the lace. The more he tapped, the more she couldn't stop remembering how he looked climbing out of the pool. Did he know what he was doing to her? The thoughts he was putting into her head? She had no business thinking of Armando this way, like a strong, desirable man. He was… Armando. Her boss. Her brother-in-law. Her future king.

And yet, his fingers kept toying with her lace sleeve, and she kept feeling beautiful, and the fantasies played in her head until the concert ended.

Until the lights in the hall brightened and she looked down at the orchestra seats only to find herself looking into the eyes of the one man capable of washing all her confidence away.

Fredo.

Armando noticed the moment the smile disappeared from Rosa's face. It was inevitable, seeing how he couldn't stop stealing glances at her all night long. He'd always considered her attractive, but tonight was different. With her hair clipped loosely at her neck, and that dress… She had to stop wearing those damn blazers and sweater sets. A body like hers, all soft curves made for a man to run his hands down, should never be hidden. Of course, he'd always known she had a good figure. What surprised him was that he was thinking about hands and curves. Apparently he wasn't as sexually dead as he thought.

Now he followed her line of sight, zooming in on Fredo Marriota immediately. Rosa's former husband was looking up at her with an expression of surprise and disbelief. Armando watched as, despite having a date of his own, the man openly assessed Rosa's appearance. It was clear seeing Rosa in the royal box irritated him. His stare was callous and sharp and made Armando's jaw clench.

At first, Rosa appeared to shrink under her ex's scrutiny, reminding Armando of the conversation he'd overheard at the shelter. Her display of weakness lasted only for a moment, because the next thing he knew, she'd reached inside herself and found a backbone. Her shoulders straightened, and she met Fredo stare for haughty stare.

Shooting Fredo a side glance of his own, Armando made a point of slipping his hand around Rosa's waist and pulling her tight to his side. "Well played," he whispered. From Fredo's vantage point, it must have looked like he was nuzzling her neck, since the man immediately blanched. "I had no idea he would be here."

"Me neither. But then again, this is a large networking event, so I shouldn't be surprised."

"He doesn't look very happy to see the two of us together."

"It has more to do with seeing me in a capable position," Rosa replied. "What are you doing?"

He'd leaned close again, so he could talk in her ear. "Playing with him." The man could use a reminder of what he'd lost. "Every time I lean close, his eyes bulge like a frog's, or haven't you noticed?"

"I noticed. So has everyone else in the theater, for that matter. How will you explain to Mona if your picture ends up in tomorrow's paper?"

Mona, whom he hadn't thought about

once since Rosa opened her front door. "She will understand," he replied.

"Are you sure? I don't want to cause trouble between you."

And Armando wanted to put Fredo in his place. She moved to break free; he held her tight.

"I am positive," he said. "I hardly think Mona's the jealous type." One of the reasons he'd selected her was her decidedly implacable nature. "Your ex-husband, however, looks as though someone stole his favorite toy." Reaching up, he pretended to brush a stray hair from her cheek. *To make Fredo seethe,* he said to himself. Still, he felt an unfamiliar tightening at how her skin turned pink where his fingers touched.

"Insulted, more likely. I'm sure in his mind, I attended with you on purpose just so I could make him look foolish."

"But that's…"

"Ridiculous? Not to him. Do you mind if we leave now? The car is probably waiting out front." She turned in his grip so that her back faced the orchestra, essentially dismissing the man they'd been talking about.

Trying to dismiss the topic altogether, Armando suspected.

"Of course." Casting one final look over her shoulder, he guided her from the box to the door where Vittorio and other members of the royal contingent waited patiently.

"Will His Majesty be heading anywhere else this evening?" Vittorio asked as they passed.

"Just home," Rosa answered for them, forgetting she wasn't his assistant tonight. "I mean, my apartment building first, and then His Highness will be heading home."

"Actually…" Armando took another look behind him before looking back at Rosa. Despite her proud stance, the standoff with Fredo had taken a toll. The glow she'd maintained all evening had faded. He hated seeing her evening end on such a sour note. "We will both be returning the palace."

"We will? Why?"

He smiled. Was it a trick of the light or were Rosa's eyes always this soft and brown? What would they look like lit by hundreds of Christmas lights? Would they sparkle like chocolate diamonds?

He would find out soon enough.

"Royal decree," he teased in answer to her question.

Her eyes narrowed. "What does that mean?"

"It means it is a surprise."

Normally, Armando wasn't one for surprises. It had been years since he did anything remotely spontaneous, and while in the scope of things, this surprise wasn't anything dramatic, he still found himself energized by the idea. He couldn't remember the last time he'd been excited. Bouncing on the balls of his feet, rapid pulse excited. Yet here he was, wrapped in a haze of exhilaration.

All over what was really something very silly. Didn't matter. He still looked forward to his plan.

Because he wanted to be sure Rosa's evening ended on a positive note.

It had nothing to do with wanting to see her eyes under Christmas lights.

"Have I told you that I do not like surprises?" Rosa remarked when the car pulled into the underground entrance behind the palace.

"Since when?" he replied. "I seem to recall you and your sister planning all sorts of surprises together before she and I got married."

"Correction, Christina planned surprises. I was there solely for support and labor. My life was unpredictable enough. The last thing I needed was more unpredictability."

He didn't answer until the driver had opened the door and they stepped onto the pavement. "Unpredictable. You mean Fredo." Her comments from earlier had stayed with him. They, along with the comments she'd made to Max at the shelter, were forming a very ugly picture.

Her steps stuttered. "I don't want to talk about Fredo right now," she said, looking to her shoes.

She never did, Armando wanted to say. That she continued to shut down the conversation when he asked hurt. Childish, he knew, but he needed her to open up to him. Why wouldn't she? They were family, were they not?

Except the appreciation running through him as he watched her walk ahead of him didn't feel very familial. All women should move so fluidly.

Good Lord, but his thoughts were all over the map this evening.

At least he wasn't the only one having appreciative thoughts, he said to himself as he caught the overnight guard stealing a glance in Rosa's direction. Yet again, his mind went back to Fredo, and he wondered what was wrong with the man that he could find fault with a woman as likable and attractive as Rosa.

Looking at her now, standing by the elevator with a bag clutched to her chest, her gaze contemplative and distant, something inside him lurched. She really was beautiful.

"I'm sorry if I upset you," he said. Thus far, the excursion wasn't going as planned.

"No, I'm the one who should apologize. Here you are trying to do something nice, and I'm being difficult."

Unlike at the concert hall when he'd pretended in front of Fredo, this time there was real hair clinging to her cheek. Armando brushed it free with the back of his hand. "You couldn't be difficult if you tried."

"I hope you don't expect me to say neither are you," she replied, ducking her head.

"Why not? It wouldn't kill you to lie, would it?"

"Possibly."

Normally, the banter diffused any tension that was between them, but this time, the air remained thick as they stepped on the elevator. Armando wasn't completely surprised. A strange atmosphere had been swirling around them all evening.

At nearly four hundred years old, the grand palace of Corinthia could be broken into two major sections—the original front section, which was open to the public, and the royal residence and offices, which resided in the more modern rear section. When the elevator doors opened, Rosa instinctively headed toward the offices. Chuckling, he grabbed her hand and tugged her toward the original castle.

"Okay, I admit I'm curious now," she said. "Isn't this section of the building closed this time of night?"

"To the public. It is never closed to me. Come along."

In the center, a quartet of stairways came together in a large open area known as the grand archway. Armando literally felt a thrill as he led her toward one of the staircases. Below them, the floor below the archway was pitched in blackness.

"Now," he said, pausing, "I need you to wait here and close your eyes."

"And then what? You will push me down the stairs?"

"I might, if you don't do what I say."

He waited until she obliged, then hurried down the darkened stairwell. Thankfully, years of childhood explorations left him with indelible memories of every nook and cranny. He located everything in a matter of minutes. When he finished, he positioned himself at the bottom of the stairs.

"All right," he called up. "Open your eyes."

Rosa's gasp might have been the most beautiful noise he had heard in a very long time.

CHAPTER SIX

HE'D LIT THE Corinthian Christmas tree.

Rosa had seen the official tree many times in her life, but this was the first time she'd ever seen the archway illuminated solely by Christmas lights. She gazed in marvel at the towering Italian spruce. The theme this year was red and gold, and somehow the decorator had managed to find golden Christmas lights. As a result, the entire archway was bathed in the softest yellow.

From his spot at the bottom of the stairs, Armando smiled at her. "What do you think? Do you still not like surprises?" he asked.

Rosa's answer caught in her throat. Standing there in the golden glow of the trees, he looked a tuxedoed Christmas god, beautiful and breathtaking.

"Amazing," she whispered. She didn't mean the lights.

"You missed the ceremony the other night, so I thought I would treat you to a private one. I realize as surprises go, it's a little underwhelming…"

"No." She hurried down to join him. "It's perfect."

He'd lit more than the tree. The phalanx of smaller trees that stood guard around the main one sparkled with lights, too, as did the garlands hanging from the balustrade.

"I had to skip the window candles," he told her. "They're too hard to light without a step stool."

"I'll forgive you."

Unbelievable. She sank down on the bottom step to better study the room. This was the first time she'd seen this space so quiet. Because it was the palace hub, the archway was a continual stream of noise and people. Sitting here now, in the solitude, felt more like she was in an enchanted forest filled with thousands of golden stars. There was a feeling of timelessness in the air. Watching the shadows on the stone walls, it was easy to imagine the spirits of Armando's ancestors floating back and forth among the trees. Generations of Santoros connected by tradition for eternity.

And he'd created the moment for *her*. As if she were someone important. The notion left her breathless.

"Why..." she started.

"I didn't want your encounter with Fredo to be how you ended your evening. So now, it can end with Christmas trees instead."

Rosa's insides were suddenly too full for her body. She was being overly romantic, getting emotional over a simple kindness.

But then, there'd been so many simple kindnesses tonight, hadn't there.

Armando wedged himself between her and the banister and stretched his legs out in front of him. "When my sister and I were children, we would sneak in here after everyone went to bed and light the trees," he said. "When it came to Christmas, Arianna was out of control. She couldn't get enough of the Christmas lights."

"Neither could you, it sounds like."

He shook his head. "You know Arianna.

She acts first and thinks later. I had to go along if only to keep her from getting into trouble. Did you know she used to insist on sneaking into our parents' salon to try and catch Babbo Natale every year? I spent every Christmas worried she was going to knock over the tree on herself or something."

Rosa smiled. "Taking responsibility even then."

His sigh was tinged with resignation. "Someone had to."

The Melancholy Prince, thought Rosa. Told as a child he carried the responsibility for a nation. When, she wondered, was the last time he had done something purely because doing so made him happy? She already knew the answer: he'd married her sister. While Christina was alive, he had at least shown glimpses of a brighter, lighter self. Now that side of him only appeared when Rosa arm-twisted him into situations that required it. Like playing Babbo.

Until tonight. Even though at his age lighting the palace couldn't be called mischievous, his face had a brightness she hadn't seen in years. You could barely see the shadows in his blue eyes. The look especially suited him. If she could, Rosa would encourage him to play every night.

Again, he had done this *for her*.

"Thank you." She put her hand on his knee and hoped he could feel the depth of her appreciation in her touch.

"You're welcome." Maybe he did know, because he covered her hand with his.

"Christina and I used to wait up for Babbo, too," she said, looking up at the twinkling treetop. "Her idea, of course. I was always afraid he would be mad and switch us to the naughty list. I don't know why, since Christina would have talked our way out of it." No one could resist her sister, not even Santa Claus.

"True." He nudged her shoulder. "Your arm-twisting skills aren't half-bad, either. I bet you could have done some sweet talking, too."

"No, I would have stuttered and fumbled my words. I would have been the one who fell down the stairs, too. I might still, if I'm not careful. Grace is not my middle name."

Armando drew back with a frown. "Are you kidding? You're one of the most graceful women I've ever met."

"I—I am?"

"You should watch yourself walk out of a room sometime."

"You do know, now that you've said something, I'll never walk unconsciously again?"

"Sorry."

"No, I am. Putting myself down is a bad habit. I'm getting better, but conditioning takes time to overcome. Hear something enough times, and it becomes a part of you."

"Yes, it does," he replied. Like Armando and responsibility.

Together, they sat in silence. Rosa could feel the firmness of Armando's thigh against hers. Taking its cue from the hand resting atop hers, the contact marked her insides with warmth that was simultaneously thrilling and soothing. She selfishly wished Fredo would appear again so that she might feel Armando pull her tight in his arms, the way he had at the concert hall, and indulge in even more contact.

Instead, he did her one better.

"Fredo is an ass," he muttered, and she stiffened, afraid he'd read her thoughts. "I know," he said. "You don't want to talk about him, but I have to say it. The guy is a class-A jerk."

She could end the discussion right there by not saying a word, but the indignation in his voice on her behalf deserved some type of comment. "Yes, he is, although he can be charming when he needs to be."

"They always are. Isn't that what they told us at the shelter? It's why a lot of very intelligent women who should know better find themselves trapped."

A woman who should know better. That certainly described her. Rosa could feel Armando holding back his curiosity. Trying so hard to honor her request in spite of the questions running through his head.

From the very start of their friendship, he'd treated her with kindness and respect. More than any man she'd known. Most people—her parents, even—thought she was crazy to leave a wealthy, successful man like Fredo; they couldn't understand why she wouldn't be happy. But Armando had never judged her. Never asked what she thought she was doing. He trusted that she had a reason.

Perhaps it was time she offered him a little trust in return.

"I never told anyone. About Fredo," she said softly.

"Not even Christina?"

She shook her head. "Although I think she knew I was unhappy. Thing is, for a long time I thought the problem was with me. That if I wasn't such a fat, stupid fool, my marriage would be better."

"What are you talking about? You're none of those things."

"Not according to Fredo. He never missed an opportunity to tell me I was second-rate." Looking to her lap, she studied the patterns playing out in the lace. Tiny red squares that formed larger red squares, which then formed ever larger squares. She traced one of the holes with her index finger. "Didn't help that Christina was everything that I wasn't. I loved my sister, but she was so beautiful…"

"So are you."

Armando's answer made her breath catch. "You are," he repeated when she looked at him. "Your face, your eyes, your figure. The way you walk…"

"Regardless," she said, looking back to her lap. She wasn't trying to fish for compliments, even if his comments did leave her insides warm and full enough to squeeze tears.

"The point is for a long time I believed him. Same way I believed him when he reminded me how fortunate I was that he was willing to take me off my father's hands."

"I'm going to shoot the bastard," Armando muttered.

It was an extreme but flattering response. Rosa found herself fighting back a smile. "There's no need. Your performance tonight wounded him more than enough."

Armando shook his head. "He deserves worse. If I'd known—"

"Don't," she said, grasping his hands in hers. This time he wasn't talking about her not sharing, but about his not stepping in to defend her. She wouldn't have him feeling guilty because her shame kept her from speaking up. "I told you, I didn't want anyone to know."

"But why not? I could have helped you."

"You and Christina were in the middle of this great romance—I didn't want to ruin the mood with my problems. And then, after Christina died, you were grieving. It wasn't the time. Besides…" Here was the true answer. "I was ashamed."

"You had nothing to be ashamed about."

Didn't she? "Do you know how hard it is to admit you spent nearly a decade allowing someone to strip you of your self-respect because you thought you deserved it?" Even now, the regret choked her like bile when she thought of the power Fredo had held over her. Power she'd given him. A tear slipped from the corner of her eye. She moved to swipe the moisture away only to have Armando's thumb pass across her skin first. When he was finished, his hand remained, his palm cupping her cheek. "No one ever deserves to be abused," he said.

"I told you, Fredo never struck me."

"You know as well as I do abuse doesn't always come from a fist."

So her counselor always told her. Words could cut deep, too.

Armando's touch was warm and comforting, calling to her to lean in and absorb its promised strength. "Took me a long time to learn that," she said. "I figured as long as I wasn't sporting a black eye, I didn't have a right to complain. Besides, when it was happening…" Her voice caught. How she hated talking about those years out loud. Admitting she thought she deserved everything Fredo did and said.

Armando's fingers slid from her cheek to her jaw, lifting her face so their eyes would stay connected. The smile he gave her was gentle and understanding. It told her that he wouldn't ask for details.

Knowing she had a choice gave her the strength to say more.

"It catches you by surprise, you know? At first, it's subtle. Constructive criticism. An outburst over something you did that doesn't seem worth fighting about, because, well, maybe you didn't communicate well enough. Meanwhile, your parents are telling you how lucky you are that such a successful, handsome man wanted to be with you, and you start to think, *he's so charming and agreeable with everyone else—it has to be my fault.* That you are the one letting him down by being inferior."

Armando squeezed her knee. "You are not—"

"I am also not Christina," she said, anticipating his protest.

The feel of his touch against her skin was too enticing, so she turned her face away. As his hand dropped, a chill rushed in to fill its absence. She stared at the Christmas lights. "Life is not always easy when your baby sister is a great beauty," she told him. "Soon as she walked in the room, I ceased to exist."

"That is not true."

"Isn't it?" She had to smile, weak as it was, at Armando's protest. He, the man who fell in love with Christina the moment he laid eyes on her. "The day you met her, at the reception, did you know I was standing with her?"

He stiffened. "That was different."

No, it wasn't. "You were not the first person to lose their heart at first sight, 'Mando.

Just the first one whose feelings she reciprocated."

They fell silent again. Out of the corner of her eye, she saw Armando studying his hands, a scowl marring his profile. "Do not feel bad. It was just the way things were. Christina was extraordinary." Whereas Rosa was merely average, a fact she was only now starting to realize was a perfectly fine thing to be. Not everyone could be Christina. To hold a grudge against her sister for being special would have been a waste of energy.

For some reason, talk of her sister's superiority made her think of Mona, another winner in the beauty and character lotto. Someone else with whom Rosa couldn't compete. Not that there was a competition.

Next to her, Armando shifted his weight on the stone step. "You really believed Fredo was the best you could do?"

"Silly, I know." Shameful was more like it. That a bully like Fredo was able to chip away at her self-esteem the way he did. "But Fredo had me convinced I would be a lonely nothing without him. Not only was he doing me a favor by being my husband, but I had no other options. Everything I had—money, a home—were because of him. If I left, I would have nothing."

"What made you change your mind?"

"Strange as it sounds, it was Christina's accident," she told him. "I was sitting at her bedside, holding her hand, thinking how unfair it was that someone like her, whose life was wonderful, should die when there were so many like me who could go in her place, and suddenly, I heard her voice in my head. You know that voice she used when she got exasperated."

Armando gave a soft chuckle. "I certainly do."

"Well, that voice told me life was too short and unpredictable to waste time being miserable, so take back control. So I divorced Fredo as soon as I could."

His hand found hers again. "I'm glad," he whispered.

"Me, too." Who knew where she would be if she had not? Certainly not sitting on the steps in a lace ball gown surrounded by an enchanted palace wonderland. Armando would be but a distant part of her life. Her insides started to ache. The idea of a life without Armando was…was…

Right around the corner. The thought struck her, hard. Mona would be taking him away forever.

Before she realized, there was moisture rimming her eyes. "I'm sorry," she said, sniffing the tears back. "Here you are trying to end the evening on a happy note, and I go and spoil it by acting maudlin."

"You didn't spoil anything. I'm honored you trusted me enough to finally tell me."

"Trust was never the issue, Armando. I told you, I was ashamed. And afraid," she added in a small voice.

"Afraid? Of me?"

She closed to her eyes. "Of seeing pity in your eyes." That last thing she wanted was Armando looking at her like a victim. She couldn't bear it.

"Never in a million years," she heard him say. A wonderful promise, but… She squeezed her eyes tighter.

"Rosa, look at me." Rosa couldn't. She didn't want to know what she might see.

But Armando was persistent. Capturing her face in his hands, he forced her out of hiding. "Rosa, look at me," he urged. "Look me in the eye. Do you see pity?"

Slowly, she lifted her lids. Armando was gazing at her with eyes blue and nonjudgmental. "I would sooner cut them out than look at you with anything less than admiration."

"Little dramatic, don't you think?"

"Not in this case. What you did took courage, Rosa. Courage and strength. If anyone needs to fear judging, it's me for not being worthy of your friendship."

"You'll always be worthy," she whispered. This time, it was she who reached across the space to touch his face. His cheeks were rough with the start of an early beard. For some reason, the sensation aroused her, as if the whiskers were scratching inside her and not her skin. She wondered if her touch had shifted something inside him as well, because the blue began to take on different shades. What had been light was slowly growing dark and hooded.

"You're wrong."

Focused on the shifting of his eyes, Rosa nearly missed his words. "Wrong?"

"Thinking you're not special. You couldn't be more wrong. You're smart, strong. Beautiful." It'd been too long since someone had said such lovely words to her, and the way Armando said them was so sincere that Rosa melted with pleasure.

"I wasn't looking for compliments," she said.

"Not compliments. Truth."

Rosa nearly sighed aloud at his answer. The moment must going to her head, she decided. Why else would she think Armando's gaze had dropped to her mouth? Or long for him to move closer?

"We—" She started to say that they should say good-night, but her mind was distracted by the way Armando's lips curled into a smile. He whispered something. It sounded like Fredo was an idiot, but she couldn't be sure. Next thing she knew, those beautiful curved lips were pressed against hers.

Rosa's breath caught.

Her heart stopped.

Her eyes fluttered shut, and her hand slid

to the curls at the back of his head. Sweet and lingering, it was a kiss worthy of a fairy tale. Only it was Armando whose lips were gently coaxing a response. Armando whose fingers trailed down her neck to caress the base of her throat.

A moment later, he pulled away, leaving her dazed and confused. *What...?*

"Mistletoe," he said, pointing upward. "Be a shame to ignore tradition."

Dazed and mute, Rosa simply nodded. Looking up, she saw nothing. If the mistletoe was there, it was hidden in shadows.

Armando lifted her hair off her shoulder, tucking it neatly to the base of her neck. His smile was enigmatic. There was emotion playing in the depths of his gaze, but what it was, Rosa couldn't tell. She wasn't used to seeing anything but sadness in his eyes, so perhaps it too was the shadows playing tricks.

In a way, she felt like the whole evening had been one giant illusion from the moment Armando knocked on her door. Everything had been too romantic, too close to perfect to be anything else. For five wonderful hours, he'd made her feel desirable and special. Like a princess. There was no way those feelings could last. As soon as she said good-night, reality would return.

The question was, would their relationship return to normal as well? Or would this newfound awareness continue to simmer inside her?

"It's getting late," Armando said. "We should get you home."

And there it was—reality. Armando was already standing, a hand out to help her to her feet. Although she tried to fight it, desire pooled in the pit of Rosa's stomach the moment his fingers closed around hers, answering her question.

"Are you all right?"

Naturally, he would notice and show concern. Her fantasy evening wouldn't be complete otherwise.

"Everything's perfect," she replied. Except for one tiny problem, that was.

She'd just realized she was falling for him.

Armando called for the car to be brought around, then accompanied Rosa downstairs.

Back in the bright light, he saw that the front of her hair had worked loose from its clip, the result of their kiss. The strands begged to be brushed away from her skin, and he had to clench his fists rather than give in to the temptation.

The driver was waiting when they stepped outside. Upon seeing them, he opened the door and snapped to attention. "Your Highness." He sounded surprised.

"Just walking Rosa out," Armando replied. For a second, he had the crazy idea of joining her on the ride, but steeled himself against that temptation as well. There was no telling what he might do pressed against her in the darkened backseat.

As it was, he had to go upstairs and make sure there really was mistletoe.

"I'll see you Monday?" he asked instead.

"Of course."

"And no more avoiding each other?"

You couldn't blame him for asking. The last time, just mentioning her marriage had her dodging him for days. Who was to say what this last conversation might cause. Especially considering her expression—part dazed and part shadowed.

Mirrored how he felt inside.

They exchanged good-nights, then the driver closed the door. As Armando watched the rear lights disappear into the darkness, he kicked himself for not stealing another kiss.

What excuse would he give, though? There was definitely no mistletoe hanging above them this time, and "I want to be close to you" sounded too much like a line, even if it was true.

The kiss upstairs had been born from admiration. When they were establishing the shelter, he'd heard story after story of women who found the strength to walk away despite being told by their abusive husbands that they would never survive on their own. To leave and start over took real courage. But then, he'd always known Rosa was strong. Hell, he'd been drawing on her strength for three years.

She was wrong, too. Years of verbal debasement were abuse; she might not have had bruises, but she'd been hurt nonethe-

less. Fredo's rising financial career had just
ground to a halt. No way would Armando
reward the man after what he did. Telling
Rosa she was an embarrassment? Killing her
self-esteem? If only he could throw people
in the dungeon.

"Pardon me, Your Highness. Is something
wrong? It's just that you've been standing in
the middle of the driveway for a while now,"
his security guard added when Armando
turned to look at him, "and I was—"

"Lost in thought," Armando replied. First
Daniela, now the guard. What was it about
his kissing Rosa that required people to ask
if he was all right?

On the other hand, both times had left
him off balance. It felt like something was
shifting inside him—something deeper than
sexual attraction. There was a yearning inside him that hadn't been there before, and,
incredible as it sounded, Rosa was the trig-
ger. If he didn't know better, he would think
he was developing feelings for her.

Impossible. He'd already had the love of
his life. His heart was buried with her. He
hadn't felt anything for three years. Tonight

was simply a product of traumatic confessions and Christmas lights. Nothing more. Turning on his heel, he headed back inside.

There had better be mistletoe hanging in that archway.

CHAPTER SEVEN

THE NEXT MORNING, instead of Christmas shopping like she planned, Rosa left her local coffee shop and headed for the palace. She needed a bit of grounding. After Armando had walked her to the car, she'd spent the entire ride home, not to mention most of the early hours, trying not to relive their kiss. No matter how hard she focused on other things, the memory of Armando's lips pressed to hers kept forcing its way to the front. For crying out loud, she even tasted him in her dreams.

Wasn't it just her luck? Three years of longing for someone to awaken the woman inside her, and it was Armando, the one man in Corinthia miles beyond her reach. If she didn't have interest in dating before, how would she ever now, having experienced the gold standard of kisses?

Which was why she needed a second shot of reality, to hammer home the fact that last night was nothing but a fantasy.

Despite the early hour, the lights in the grand archway were already lit in preparation for the day's tours. Or maybe Armando never turned them off. Either way, the arrival of day had washed away last night's magic. Whatever spirits had been dancing along the walls were back in hiding as well, giving Armando and the rest of the royal family a rest from their presence.

The sight of plain gray walls put Rosa on firmer mental ground. Gripping the balustrade, she peered upward to find a sprig of green and berries hanging from the chandelier.

Did she really think there wouldn't be?

"Rosa?"

So much for grounded. One word from the familiar voice and her stomach erupted in a swarm of butterflies. Looking over her shoulder, she saw Armando walking toward her. Seemed impossible, but he looked more handsome than he did last night. His faded jeans and black turtleneck sweater were a far cry from the tuxedo, but he wore them as with the same elegance. Casual was a look he did well. Pity his subjects didn't get to see him like this—women would be storming the gate.

The closer he got, the faster the butterflies flapped. "What are you doing here?" he asked. "I thought you took the weekend off to finish your Christmas shopping."

"I left my list in my office," she lied. "Can't very well shop without one. Well, I could, but I might forget someone. Or something. What about you?" she asked, quickly changing subjects before her babbling got out of control. "What has you wandering the halls this early in the morning?"

"Oh, you know," he said with a shrug. "Paperwork, royal proclamations. Not to mention Arianna and her wedding planners have taken over the royal residence."

"In other words, you are hiding out."

"Precisely. If I stay, I'm liable to be asked my opinion on embossed napkins. My future brother-in-law can deal with that stress on his own.

"It's not the same during the day, is it?" he said, helping himself to the coffee cup in her hand. "The tree loses something when the lights are on."

Right. The tree. For a moment, she'd been distracted by the way his lips curled around the foam. If he kissed her now, she would taste the coffee on them. "Definitely. But then, most things aren't." She wondered if the rule applied to kisses, too. If Armando were to lean in right now, would she feel the same swirl of desire? Considering the way her insides buckled over watching him drink coffee, she was pretty sure the answer was yes.

Armando's lips glistened with liquid. "I'll tell you what's not the same," he said with a frown. "Coffee without sugar. I thought you were going to stop this diet nonsense."

"There's nothing wrong with watching your weight."

"Drinking bad coffee is not weight watching, it's torture. I forbid you from doing it anymore."

"I've got a better idea. Drink your own coffee," she said, snatching back her cup. The banter felt good. She'd been afraid last night might taint their friendship.

At least it felt good until she went to take a sip and realized her lips were touching the same spot as his. Instantly, the butterflies returned.

"By the way, I—I had a great time last night," she said.

"So you said last night."

She knew that, but talking seemed a far better alternative to her other impulse, which was running her tongue along the cup rim.

"I just wanted to make sure you know how much," she said.

"I had a good time, too." To her surprise, pink inched along his cheekbones. "I was afraid you might regret opening old wounds…"

"No, not at all. In a weird way, telling you was liberating. I never realized how much the secret was weighing on me." Or rather, the shame of it. "Thank you, by the way, for not thinking me a complete failure."

"You're not a failure, period. Your taste in

men could be a little better…I mean, I could have told you Fredo was a poor choice. For starters, the man eats far too much garlic."

"Yes, he does," Rosa laughed. "And too much dairy. What was I thinking?" Her smile faded. "Sometimes I could kick myself for being so stupid," she said.

"Not stupid. Naive, maybe, but never stupid." When he said it, she believed him. Maybe last night's magic hadn't completely dissipated after all.

The sounds of footsteps floated up from below. Beneath them, security guards were readying the archway for the public. Armando leaned his forearms on the stone railing. Rosa joined him, cradling her coffee and watching the activity on the first floor.

"Clearly there is only one solution," he said after a moment.

"Solution?"

"Regarding your terrible taste. From now on, you'll have to run all your potential dates by me, and I will decide if they are worthy of you."

"Is that so?" He was joking, but Rosa's

spirits sagged slightly nonetheless. A tiny part of her had been hoping last night's kiss…

"Absolutely," he continued. "You're going to need my discerning eye. We don't want you falling for any old line. Just the ones I like." The sparkle in his eyes belied his seriousness. "I have to warn you, though. I have exceedingly high standards. In fact…" He pressed his shoulder against hers, and the wave of warmth that passed through her almost made her drop her coffee. "There is a very good chance I won't find anyone suitable at all."

"Is that so?"

"No. Very few men will measure up, as far as I'm concerned."

"None at all?" she asked.

His gaze aligned with hers. Between the shadows and his pupils, Rosa could barely make out the blue. "Maybe one or two," he replied.

She suddenly had trouble swallowing, the air from her lungs having stopped midway in her throat. "One would be enough," she managed to say. Had his pupils gotten even larger? The blue had been completely obliterated.

"One, then," he replied. "One very qualified candidate."

"Very qualified?"

"The best." Rosa didn't know a few inches could be so far away until Armando leaned in toward her. They were in their own private space. "We're standing underneath the mistletoe again," he whispered. "You know what that means…"

Most definitely. What's more, this time, there was no crowd or midnight confession to spur the moment forward. Just them. She parted her lips.

Armando's phone rang.

"You should answer," Rosa replied when he groaned. "It could be your father."

"If it is, he has horrible timing."

Still, no one in Corinthia ignored a phone call from the king, not even his son, so he reached into his breast pocket. One look at his expression told Rosa the caller wasn't King Carlos.

"It's Mona," Armando replied. There

wasn't enough room in his eyes to hold their apology. "I'm sorry."

Rosa wasn't. As far as she was concerned, Mona's timing couldn't be more perfect. It saved her from making a very foolish mistake. So foolish, she almost laughed out loud.

With the walls of the archway closing in, she turned and hurried down the stairs. Once outside, she kept hurrying, through the front gate and down the block, stopping only when she reached the same coffee shop where she began.

Collapsing against the brick facade, she closed her eyes and told herself her heart was racing from exertion and not from the feelings swirling around inside her.

We're standing underneath the mistletoe again...

Heaven help her, she wanted to go back. Didn't matter if it was foolish or if Armando was making a joke, she wanted to go back, stand beneath that mistletoe and wait for Armando to take her in his arms.

She wanted him.

How? When did everything change? When

did he stop being Armando, the man who married her sister, and become simply Armando the man? Last night amid the Christmas lights? Or earlier? Thinking back, Armando had always been one of two measures by which she rated others—Fredo at the low end and Armando at the top—and she'd told herself that when she decided she was ready to date, she would shoot for someone in the middle. After all, while she might not be the lump of clay Fredo thought her to be, she knew better than to put herself at Armando's level, either. So what did she do? Fall for Armando anyway. Could she be a bigger idiot?

Banging her head against the brick, she let out a loud sigh. Armando had just said she had terrible taste in men.

If only he knew.

Armando tried his best to focus on the voice talking on the other end of the line and not on the red-coated figure heading down the stairs.

"I wanted to apologize for missing the concert," Mona was saying. "I thought I would be well enough to travel, but I still have a fever. The doctor is afraid I might be contagious."

"Then it was definitely a good idea to stay home," Armando replied.

"Perhaps, but I am still sorry. I know how important this event is to you."

"There is no need to apologize. You can't control what your body is going to do." Sometimes your body wanted you to kiss a woman senseless. Confessions and Christmas lights, huh? What was his excuse this morning? Because he wanted to kiss her as badly as ever.

More than kiss her. He wanted to wrap her in his arms and not let go.

Below him, he saw Rosa crossing the tile, and his body clutched in frustration. He wanted to call for her to stop, but Mona was still talking.

"I swear I am normally very healthy. The doctor says this is one of the worst strains of flu he's ever seen," Mona was saying. "But I am definitely on the upswing, and will be one hundred percent as soon as possible. You have my word."

You have my word. Mona's statement was the perfect antidote to the spell that had gripped him as well as a reminder that Armando had made a promise of his own. "I'm looking forward to it," he replied, gripping the phone a little tighter. Rosa, meanwhile, had disappeared through the exit, leaving the archway cold and quiet. Just as well. "I also should be the one apologizing." For many things. "I didn't realize you were as sick as you are."

"I downplayed the situation when we spoke. I had the idea that if I told myself I was healthy, I would get healthy. Unfortunately..." She paused to cough. When she spoke again, her voice was raspy. "Unfortunately, I was wrong."

She certainly sounded terrible, Armando thought guiltily. "Why don't I fly in and visit? I promise to stay out of germ range. It would give us a chance to spend time together." Not to mention putting some distance between him and Rosa. Hypocritical, considering he'd admonished Rosa about avoiding him not five minutes ago.

His suggestion was met with a pause.

"That is very nice of you, but I am afraid I would not be very good company. I wouldn't be able to show you around. Plus I look a sight."

"People with the flu often do," Armando noted.

"I know, but I would spend the entire visit feeling self-conscious. I hate whenever anyone sees me not looking my best."

Dear God, they were going to be man and wife. Did she think a fever and messy hair might send him running?

Armando thought of all the states he and Rosa had seen each other in, including one very embarrassing incident right after she started work when she vomited in his office waste receptacle. She'd been mortified. Spent the entire time apologizing and choking back feverish tears. Now that he remembered, she'd said she didn't want him seeing her in such a state, too. He'd ignored her. Instead, he sat by her side, rubbed circles on her back, passed her tissues and told her he was right where he belonged. "We're a team," he'd told her. "What's a little flu bug between partners?" Then he'd bundled her down the hall to one of the guest rooms, and they'd watched a movie until she fell asleep. Oddly enough, it was one of his fondest memories of their friendship.

He tried to picture rubbing Mona's back only to imagine being told to stay away.

"I would hate to think my company was causing you stress," he said, partly to the image in his head.

On the other end of the line, he heard a relieved sigh. "Thank you for understanding. We will enjoy our visit much better when I'm back to myself. Perhaps next week?"

"At the wedding?"

"That would be nice. I will let you know in a few days if I think I'll be feeling well enough so we can make arrangements."

"Sounds good." It struck him how formal and businesslike their conversation sounded. This was what he wanted, though, wasn't it? A business arrangement? A week ago he couldn't imagine thinking about anything more. His heart wasn't looking for more.

His eyes looked up at the mistletoe.

He squeezed them shut. Even if his heart

was looking for more, he couldn't. He'd made a promise, and Corinthia's reputation rested on his honoring it.

He talked to Mona for a few more minutes, about the concert and what few details he knew about Arianna's wedding, then agreed to talk later in the week. He had just disconnected when he spied his father strolling the corridor. "There you are," Carlos said. "Your sister ordered me to find you."

"Funny," he replied. "I thought you were the one in charge."

"Of Corinthia, maybe. Of the bride…" He paused. "Is any father of the bride ever in charge?"

"In other words, my sister has you wrapped around her little finger." No surprise there.

"What can I say? She is my baby girl. I want her to be happy."

It might be early, but King Carlos was dressed as dapperly as always. He'd once told Armando a king needed to be on any time he stepped outside his private quarters. "The people expect their king to act like a king," he'd said. As his father drew closer, Armando noticed the older man's jacket hung looser than it used to. Seemed as if every week, he grew a little older. The weight of pending responsibility that rested perpetually on Armando's shoulders grew a little heavier.

"Surely you didn't think you could escape unscathed," his father remarked.

"I'd hoped."

"You might as well get used to it. This is only a small ceremony. Yours and Mona's will be far more elaborate."

"Must it? We are talking about my second marriage."

"Regardless, you are the crown prince," his father replied. "The people will want to celebrate."

Right, the people. Those thousands of candles relying on him to stay lit. The universe was certainly intent on reminding him of his duties today, wasn't it?

His father clapped him on the shoulder, breaking his thoughts. "I know what you are thinking, son."

"You do?" How, when he wasn't sure himself? A week ago yes, but now? Not so much.

"But of course," the king replied. "I know better than anyone how difficult it is to move forward when what you really want is to bring back the past. I know how much you loved Christina." Armando felt a stab of guilt. He hadn't been thinking of Christina last night—or this morning. Only of Rosa.

"When your mother died, it was all I could do to hold myself together, I missed her that much."

"I know," Armando replied. All too well he remembered the sight of his father with his face buried in his hands.

"I still miss her. Every day." He gave a soft laugh. "We Santoros love hard."

"So I've been told." At least his father did. Armando didn't know what he was doing anymore.

"What I'm trying to say is that I know what you are doing is difficult. You're putting your sister's happiness—not to mention the welfare of this country—ahead of your own needs." His hand still lay on Armando's shoulder, and so he gave a squeeze. "I hope you know how grateful I am. Grateful and proud. When I step down, Corinthia will be in wonderful hands."

For an aging man, he had an amazing grip. The pressure brought moisture to Armando's eyes. "Thank you."

"No, son, thank you. Now…" Lifting his hand, his father slapped him between the shoulder blades. "Let us go see what duties your sister has assigned to us, shall we?"

"I'll be right there. I just have to make a quick phone call."

"Don't dally too long. I don't want to go looking for you again."

Armando chuckled. "Five minutes."

"I will hold you to that," his father replied, waggling a finger. "I love my daughter, but I refuse to deal with her bridal preparations by myself."

"Coward."

"Absolutely. One day you will have a daughter, and you will understand."

He was probably right. "Don't worry, you have my word." And Armando always kept his promises.

His eyes flickered to the mistletoe. Unfortunately.

* * *

Instead of going shopping like she said, Rosa ended up spending the weekend at Christina's Home, helping the residents with their Christmas baking. Working with the other women helped ground her, reminded her there were worse things in life than unrequited feelings. Seriously, what did it matter if Armando didn't return her attraction? It wasn't as if it was a surprise. She was a chubby, average personal assistant. And that wasn't her insecurity talking. Those were simply the facts. She also had a job and a place to call home, which made her better off than a lot of people. To quote Fredo, which she hated doing even when he was right, she had it pretty damn good.

She'd get over her crush or whatever it was.

By the time she returned to work on Monday, she was in a much better place. In fact, she thought as she stepped into the elevator, she'd even go so far as to say her feelings were shifting back to normal. Why not? They crept up on her overnight—who's to say they couldn't disappear just as quickly? Right?

Right?

Armando was sitting at her desk when she walked in. Wearing one of his dark suits, his tie and pocket square a perfect Corinthian red, he was busy reading her computer screen and didn't see her. Rosa's insides turned end over end anyway. "Isn't that desk a little small for you?" she asked. She was not trying to sound flirtatious; his long, lean figure dwarfed the writing table.

Nor did the way his eyes brightened when Armando looked mean anything. "I was looking for the notes on last week's meeting with the American ambassador. He's coming by this afternoon, and I deleted the copy you sent me."

"You do that a lot."

"What can I say? I don't like a crowded inbox."

"Thank goodness you have me, then." She turned to hang up her coat on the coatrack in the corner.

"I know."

Rosa paused. It was the same banter they'd exchanged dozens of times, only this time, the words sounded different. There was a note of melancholy attached to the gratitude that unnerved her. Slowly she draped her coat onto its brass hook. "It's snowing outside," she said. "I heard one of the guards say we might even see accumulation on the ground. Might be the first time in years Corinthia could have a white Christmas."

Armando was looking at her now, not the computer. She could tell because her spine felt his attention and had begun to prickle. Still afraid to turn around, she made a show out of brushing the droplets of water from the blue wool. "Is something wrong?" she asked.

"I wanted…"

Hearing his exasperated sigh, Rosa stopped fussing with her coat and turned around. It wasn't like Armando to sound this uncertain. It made her uneasy.

The contrite look on his face didn't help. "I wanted to apologize…"

Oh, Lord, he was going to tell her he was sorry for kissing her. "It's all right," she cut in. "There is no need to apologize. It's a silly holiday tradition."

"Maybe, but my behavior the other morning crossed the line. I was inappropriate, and I apologize."

In other words, he was sorry he'd made the suggestion. "That's what happens during the holidays," she said, forcing a smile. "All the celebrating makes people say things they don't mean. Don't worry, I didn't take offense."

"It's not that I didn't mean it, I just…"

Just what? Rosa knew she should ask, but she was too stuck on the first part of his sentence to say the words. Was he saying he wanted to kiss her again?

Pushing himself to his feet, he moved around to the front of the desk. "You're a beautiful woman, Rosa. What man wouldn't want to kiss you?"

"You would be surprised," she murmured.

"That is Fredo talking. Believe me, any man with half a brain would kiss you in a heartbeat."

She would have smiled at his calling Fredo stupid if he weren't filling her personal space. Rejection would be so much easier with a desk between them. Or breathing room. Anything besides the scent of his skin teasing her nostrils. "There's no need to oversell your point," she told him.

"I mean every word."

She risked looking him in the eye. "But?" There had to be a *but*. After all, for all his sweet words, he was apologizing, not taking her in his arms.

Shaking his head, Armando stepped away. "I'm not dead," he said. "I see a beautiful woman, I am going to feel desire. It's only natural."

He started pacing, a sign that he was thinking out loud. Trying hard to move past his finding her desirable, Rosa leaned back and waited for him to work out the rest of the explanation. The part that would pour cold water over the rest of his words.

"It wouldn't be fair," he said. "To kiss you. Not when I don't… That is…"

"I understand." There was no need for her to hear the words after all. She'd heard them often enough. His heart was buried with Christina. He was emotionally dead.

He might as well marry a stranger and help Corinthia, because he would never love again.

That's what he meant by it not being fair. He might want her, but his feelings didn't—couldn't—go deeper.

Then there was Mona. Even if he could care, there was Mona.

At least he cared enough to worry about leading her on. She should take solace in that. Then, his sense of honor was one of the qualities that made him so special.

The least she could do was let him off the hook. Inserting a lightheartedness she didn't feel into her voice, she asked, "Aren't you being a bit egotistical?"

Armando stopped his pacing. "I beg your pardon?"

"We were flirting under the mistletoe. You might be a good kisser, but that is still a big leap to go from a kiss to breaking my heart."

"So, you didn't feel—"

"I'm not dead," she said, throwing his answer back at him. "You're a wonderful kisser. But even I'm smart enough to know that one kiss does not a relationship make."

"That's good to know," he said, nodding. The note in his voice was embarrassed relief, Rosa told herself. It just sounded like disappointment.

"Now," she said, walking around and taking her seat, "if we are finished making needless apologies, would you like me to print out the notes for your meeting with Ambassador Wilson?"

His smile was also tinged with embarrassed relief. "Please. I'll be in my office. And, Rosa?" She looked up from her computer screen to find his eyes filled with silent communication. "Thank you."

"You're welcome." She dropped her gaze back to her screen before he could see her moist-eyed response. It had been for the best, this conversation. Better to be reminded of reality than to make a fool of herself pining for something that couldn't be.

Like she told herself when she got on the elevator, there were worse things than unrequited feelings. She couldn't think of any right now, but there were.

Didn't he feel like the proper fool? Blast his decision to keep the office door open, since right now Armando wanted to slap the back of his desk chair with all his might. Dragging a hand through his curls, he glared at the snow falling outside his window. Egotistical was right. Here he'd been worrying about whether he had been leading Rosa on and all this time she hadn't been the least concerned. From the sounds of it, she hadn't given their moments under the mistletoe a second thought.

Why the hell hadn't she? Surely she had felt the same frightening intimacy he'd felt on the stairs? Why then weren't her thoughts swirling with the same confusion and desire?

Don't look a gift horse in the mouth, 'Mando. Regardless of what Rosa did or did not feel, the arguments for his apology still applied. Rosa's lack of interest merely made closure that much easier. He should be relieved.

Check that. He was relieved, and now that matter was settled, his and Rosa's relationship could go back to the way it had always been.

"Here are your notes."

Or maybe not. Just like it had when she

entered the outer office, his insides clutched the second he looked at her. So sweet and soft, he literally ached to pull her close. Desire, it appeared, needed a little more than an apology to disappear.

He gripped the back of his chair instead. "Thank you," he said as she dropped the papers on his desk.

Her eyes barely lifted in acknowledgment. "You're welcome."

With his fingers gouging divots into the chair leather, he watched her walk to the door. "Making things easier," he repeated with each sway of her shapeless jacket.

Still, why the hell wasn't she as affected as he was?

CHAPTER EIGHT

AMAZING HOW QUICKLY time went when you weren't looking forward to something. If Rosa had been excited for Arianna's rehearsal dinner, the days before the ceremony would have dragged on, but since she was dreading the event—as well as the wedding itself—time sped by in a flurry of activity.

Before she realized, it was the night before Christmas Eve and she was standing by herself in the east dining room. While the wedding was small, it was by no means unelaborate. They would be dining tomorrow off three-hundred-year-old royal china bearing the Santoro crest. Tonight they were using the more modern state china with its fourteen-karat edging and matching tableware. The gold gleamed bright amid the red and white table linen. Arianna counted the forks. Six courses. Her cream-colored gown tightened at the thought.

She made a point of arriving early, while the rest of the party was in the chapel. If anyone asked, her purpose was to help Arianna's assistant. The real reason was because she couldn't face any kind of wedding reference with Armando in the room. Actually, she was trying to avoid thinking of Armando in terms of weddings, period. New Year's Day was only a week away. Each passing day left a tighter knot in the pit of her stomach. Nine days and Armando would be lost to her forever.

Not that she'd ever had him, as he had stumblingly reminded her on Monday. No one other than Christina would ever have him. But the day he announced his engagement? That spelled the absolute end. The minute sliver of hope to which her heart continued to cling would cease to exist. One would think its demise would be a relief— that it would be better to have no hope than an improbable sliver—but in typical Rosa fashion, it wasn't.

And so, rather than sit in the chapel and

face reminders of Armando's pending engagement, she decided to spend a few moments alone in the dining room preparing herself.

She was standing by the fireplace warming her toes when she heard the sound of approaching footsteps. A moment later, Armando entered at the far end of the room. Upon seeing her, he stopped short. "I wondered where you might be," he said. "I noticed you weren't in the chapel during the rehearsal."

Did that mean he had been looking for her? Rosa's pulse skipped in spite of herself. She needed to stop trying to read things into his comments. "I thought Louise might need help. She's had her hands full this week, what with the gifts and the preparations."

"You would think the wedding was ten times the size considering the number of people who have sent their regards. My sister will never want for silver ice tongs again."

"Nor soup tureens," Rosa replied. "At last count, she'd received three."

"I know, I saw the display in the other room." As per tradition, the gifts were lined up for guests to see. "I shudder to think what it would have looked like if the wedding was a major affair."

He'd know soon enough. His upcoming engagement hung between them, unmentioned. The conversation was reminiscent of others they'd had this week. Friendly, but with unspoken tension beneath the surface. Even their silences, normally comfortable, had an awkwardness about them.

Watching him watch the fire, she noted the black tie hanging loose around his neck. "Do you need assistance?" she asked. "With the tie?"

He glanced down. "Please," he said. "Damn thing keeps coming out crooked when I try." Rosa had to smile. "Arianna said she would help after rehearsal, but I have a feeling she will be distracted, and since you are here…"

"It's not as though I haven't done it a couple dozen times before," Rosa replied. Stepping close, she took hold of the ends and tugged them into place. The cloth was cold from being outside. His skin, however, emanated warmth. The heat buffeted her fingers, making them feel clumsy. "One of these days you're going to have to learn to do this yourself," she murmured.

"Why, when I have you to do it for me?"

"Who says I'm always going to be around?" In the middle of looping one end over another, she heard the portent in her words and fumbled. "I would think your bride would prefer she do this for you."

She felt his muscles tense. "Perhaps," he answered, rather distractedly. "But will she be as good as you?"

"Oh, I think most people are. It isn't as hard as you think."

"Or as easy," he replied.

"I'm not sure what you mean."

"Nothing." His Adam's apple bobbed up and down as he swallowed. "I imagine you'll be glad to be free of the duty. Taking care of me must get tiring after a while."

That was an odd choice of words. Rosa pulled the bow tight. "I've never minded doing things for you," she told him. In fact, it was one of the best parts of her job. She'd found a certain kind of symbiosis in taking care of him while he grieved. The more she did, the more she remembered how strong and capable she could be. Taking care of Armando had brought back part of the woman Fredo nearly erased.

She pulled the ends of the tie, then smoothed the front of his jacket. The planes of his chest were firm and broad beneath her fingers. "There," she said. "Perfect as always."

"So are you," he replied with a smile. "You look beautiful."

"My dress is too tight.

"Stop channeling Fredo. You look perfect. You always look perfect."

The sliver of hope throbbed inside her heart. He needed to stop making her feel special.

"Armando…"

"Rosa…"

They spoke at the same time, Armando reaching for her hand as she attempted to back away.

"I—" Whatever he was going to say was halted by a pair of deep voices. She managed to slip from his grip just as Max and another man strolled in.

"And you're telling me this is only one of the dining rooms?" the stranger was asking.

"One of three," Max replied.

"Damn. This place makes the Fox Club look like a fast food joint. Hello, who's this?" He smiled at Rosa. "You weren't at the rehearsal, were you? I would have remembered."

"Dial it back, cowboy. I don't need a scandal." Max clasped the man on the shoulder. "Rosa Lamberti, may I present to you my best friend, Darius Abbott. He just arrived from New York."

"Pleasure to meet you," Rosa replied, recognizing the name. "You're Max's best man, right?"

The African-American was slightly shorter than Max, but had a muscular build, the kind you might expect from a rugby player. The shoulders of his rented tux pulled tight as he lifted her hand to his lips. "They don't make them better," he replied, winking over her fingers. Rosa giggled at his outrageousness. Max's friend was a first-class flirt.

"Rosa is Prince Armando's assistant," Max told him. "She's been a huge help this week, too. Without her and Louisa, I'm pretty sure Arianna would have lost it."

"I didn't do that much," Rosa replied. "A little organizing is all."

"As usual, Rosa is underselling herself," Armando chimed in.

"Didn't I warn you, dude?" said Darius. Eyes sparkling, he leaned in toward her as though to divulge a dark secret. "I told him something about weddings make women crazy. Even good ones like Arianna."

"My sister didn't go crazy," Armando replied.

"Much," Rosa said. "Her nerves got to her at the end. But overall, she was pretty good," she added, looking over to Armando.

"Probably because she got such good help," Darius said. "I know I'm feeling calmer."

"What can I say, I have a gift."

"You certainly do."

Good Lord, but he was over-the-top. Rosa couldn't remember the last time a man—other than Armando—complimented her so audaciously. She would be lying if she didn't say she found his behavior immensely flattering.

Out of the corner of her eye, she could see Armando watching them with narrowed, disapproving eyes. Immediately she dialed back her behavior so he wouldn't be upset.

What was she doing? Max's friend was a charming, handsome man. If she wanted to flirt with him, that was her business. A little ego stroking was exactly what she could use right now.

It was definitely better than pining for Armando, who didn't—couldn't—want her.

Feeling audacious, she offered up her best charming smile. "Have you found where you're sitting yet, Darius?" she asked. "If you'd like, I can help you find your place setting. We don't assign places the same way as they do for American head tables."

"That'd be great." Darius's perfect teeth gleamed white as he grinned back. "Maybe I'll get lucky and you'll be sitting near me."

"You know what? I think that could be arranged." Hooking her hand through his crook in his elbow, she proceeded to lead him away from the group, patting herself on the back every step of the way. She didn't once turn back and look in Armando's direction. Even if he was boring holes in the back of her head.

Armando hated the American. Why did Max have to insist on his being the best man? So what if they were childhood friends? He could have been a peripheral guest; he didn't need to be front and center, grinning his perfect white teeth at everything Rosa said. And kissing her hand hello. Americans didn't kiss hands. He kept waiting for Rosa to shoot him a look over the man's outlandish behavior. Instead, she giggled and offered to find the man's seat. He was pretty certain they'd swapped placards as well, because there she was, four seats down next to him rather than by Armando's elbow, where she belonged.

"Do you plan to eat your soup or simply stir it all night?" his father asked.

Armando set his spoon down. "My apologies, Father. I'm afraid I don't have much of an appetite this evening." How could he with such completely inappropriate behavior going on?

"I'm just saying, it's weird to segregate one little fork. Put it on the left with all the others," he heard Darius remark.

Why was Rosa laughing? It wasn't that funny. Head tipped back, notes like the trill of a thrush…he thought that was the laugh she reserved for him.

"It is a shame Mona was unable to attend this evening," Father was saying.

"Yes, it is. I don't think she expected the weather to be as bad as it is in Yelgiers." On the inside, he was far less disappointed. Despite the fact the days were ticking closer to New Year's, he found himself fighting to stir interest in his future bride. He figured it was because they hadn't spent time together. After much persuasion, he had convinced her to chat by video the other evening. A perfectly nice talk during which she supported many—no, all—of his views and left him feeling strangely flat.

"She will be here in time for the ceremony tomorrow," he said.

"I look forward to seeing her as well as her father," King Carlos said. Down at the far end of the table, the sultan was happily engrossed in conversation with Armando's second cousin, who also happened to be the deputy defense minister. "I imagine you're eager to begin your formal courtship as well."

"Definitely," Armando replied. Perhaps when they met in person, there would be more of a spark.

Although if there wasn't one, he could hardly blame Mona, could he? Not when the reason for an arranged marriage was his inability to become emotionally involved. Funny that he should be worried about a spark all of sudden.

Soup became salad. He opted for wine. On the other side of Father, Arianna and Max were ignoring their guests in favor of gazing into each other's eyes. They'd been like that since Max stormed into the palace and declared his feelings. Eyes only for each other. His heart twisted with envy. He remembered what it was like to be that deeply in love, so everything around you faded when you were with that other person. To never feel lonely because you knew there was someone in this world who understood you, who recognized your flaws and cared anyway, about whom you felt the same.

Dammit, Rosa was laughing again. What was it about the American she found so amusing? Armando kissed her, and she told him he was reacting egotistically. This… Darius made a silly comment about oyster forks and she laughed as though it were the wittiest thing she ever heard.

"Poor tomato."

Arianna's maid of honor, Lady Tessa Greenwich, pointed to the salad. "I don't know what the vegetable did to upset you, but I'm glad you're mad at it and not me."

He looked down at the cherry tomato skewered on his fork. "That's what it gets for being the easiest to spear," he said.

"Here I thought you were angry with it."

"Angry? No," he replied. Just extremely irritated with people's lack of decorum. "Would you excuse me a moment?" He left the napkin next to his plate and stood up. "I'll be back a moment."

"Everything all right?" Lady Greenwich asked.

"It will be." Soon as he had a word with his assistant. As he walked by Rosa and Darius, he leaned in to her ear. "May I see you in the corridor?" he whispered. "Now?"

Naturally, she was smiling when he spoke. She turned the smile in his direction, which only fed his agitation. "Is there a problem?" she asked.

Rather than answer, he continued walking, knowing she would follow. Once in the corridor, he led her past two additional entrances. They ended up in the gallery next to the grand arch.

"What do you think you're doing?" he asked once he was certain they couldn't be overheard.

Her eyes widened, then narrowed. "What are you talking about?"

Dear God, but she looked beautiful tonight. Her silk gown looked like cream poured over her body. Even as irritated as he was, he wanted to run his hands along every curve and sensual swell.

"I'm talking about you and Max's friend," he replied. "The way you're laughing at everything he says."

"Because he's funny. Since when is that a crime?"

Since she wasn't laughing with Armando, that's when.

"Except that you're my assistant. You were supposed to be by my side in case I need anything." Not laughing it up with handsome foreigners.

"Come on, you're not that needy, are you? Are you serious? I'm four seats away, not on the other side of the country. An extra twenty feet will hardly make a difference. Besides," she added, folding her arms across her chest, "technically I'm not working. I'm here as a guest. That means I get to sit where I want."

"That doesn't mean you get to flirt with every man in the room."

"Flirt with…?" It was the first time he had ever seen her flare her nostrils. Unfolding her arms, she held her hands stiffly by her side and leaned in. "It's called enjoying myself."

"It's called flirting," Armando charged back. "Tossing your hair over your shoulder, laughing. Like a peacock showing her plumage," he muttered to the paintings on the wall. With Darius strutting in kind. Was it any wonder he'd lost his appetite?

"So what if I am?" Rosa asked, stepping up to his shoulder. "It's been a long time since a man has found me attractive."

Armando whipped his head around. "What are you talking about? I tell you that you're attractive all the time."

"I mean someone who isn't… It's nice, is all," she said. Their shoulders knocked as she pushed past him toward the archway.

Armando stalked after her. She stood with her back to him, staring up at the Christmas tree. For a moment, his annoyance faded as he lost himself in the skin exposed by the drape of her dress.

Until the way his fingers itched to trace her spine reignited it again. "It's inappropriate," he snapped. "You're making a spectacle of yourself."

"Says who?" she asked, turning.

Said him. It killed Armando to watch her encouraging Darius's attention when she had so easily brushed off his. "You're my personal assistant," he replied. "I expect you to behave with more decorum."

Again, she folded her arms. "What would you have me do, Armando? This is your sister's wedding rehearsal. Should I just ignore the man? Stop talking to him?"

That had been exactly what he wanted. Hearing the words aloud, however, he realized how unrealistic they sounded. "Just stop throwing yourself at him," he said.

Rosa inhaled deeply through her nose. Though they sparkled, her eyes had none of the warmth they'd had the other night.

"No," she said.

One word, spoken sharply like a slap. In fact, Armando's reflexes stiffened as if it was one. "I beg your pardon?" This was where she usually turned passive-aggressive, agreeing while showing her displeasure with a sarcastic *yes, Your Highness*.

"I said no," she repeated. The first time in three years that she had defied him.

It was the most arousing sight Armando had ever seen.

Taking another breath, she started walking toward him with careful, measured steps. "I'm not going to let people tell me what to do anymore. Not Fredo. Not you…"

"I am not Fredo," Armando shot out. "Do not compare me to that bottom dweller."

"Then stop acting like him!" she snapped back. "So long as I don't hurt anyone, who I find attractive and who I don't is none of your business. Now if you'll excuse me."

Armando grabbed her wrist. He regretted it as soon as she stiffened, but the agitation in his stomach had reached epic proportions. All he could picture was Darius's handsome face and his big hands curling over those creamy shoulders. "Are you planning to kiss him?" he asked.

"That's none of your—"

But he wouldn't be deterred. Some perverse part of him needed to know. "You just said you found him attractive. Does that mean you're planning to kiss him?"

"Maybe I am," she replied, yanking her arm free. "And so what? Unlike you, I can care again. Just because you've declared yourself dead doesn't mean I have to."

"Then you are planning to kiss him."

"Whether I do or don't is none of your business."

Armando wasn't sure if it was the assertiveness or the imaginings assaulting his brain, but he couldn't let her go. Grabbing her wrist a second time, he pulled her close. Caught off guard, her body fell into his, enabling him to slip his free arm around her waist.

"Let me go," she said.

The gentleman inside him was about to when he looked into her eyes. Beautiful, fiery eyes demanding answers. And all of a sudden, he had them. The emotions that had been swirling inside him since the concert came together with astonishing clarity. Before he could stop himself, he leaned in to kiss her.

She jerked her head back. "What do you think you're doing?"

"I—" He was acting on instinct. "I'm sorry."

Breaking their embrace, he walked over to the stairway and sat down, the irony of the location not lost on him. With his eyes focused on the floor, he listened to the sounds of Rosa straightening her dress. "I want you," he said simply.

She let out a noise that sounded like a

snort. "Seriously?" she said. "Five days ago you stood in your office and apologized for wanting me, said you weren't being fair to me. And now all of a sudden you're doing everything you apologized about?"

"I know. My actions don't make much sense."

"They don't make any sense, Armando."

Seeing her standing there so gloriously indignant, Armando's stomach lurched. How could he have been so blind? "I only realized myself," he said.

"Realized what?"

"How much I care."

The color drained from her cheeks. "Care?" Her voice cracked with emotion as she repeated the word. The sound forced Armando to his feet, but when he reached out, she held up her hand. "For three years, I've listened to how your heart was buried with Christina."

"I thought it was." In fact, if someone had asked him eight hours ago, he would have given that very answer. "Then tonight, when I saw you and Darius…"

"That's your possessiveness talking," she

said. "I've seen it before. Darius paid attention to me, so suddenly you decide you don't want to share. Then, soon as his interest wanes…" She shrugged.

"No." Damn Fredo. No doubt her ex was responsible for that kind of thinking. "I mean, yes," he continued. "I won't lie. I wanted to break Darius's finger every time he touched you. But my jealousy was only the final piece of the puzzle. What I'm feeling inside…"

She was facing away from him. Seemed that was her favorite position tonight, giving him the cold shoulder. Curling his hands around those shoulders, he buried his nose in her hair for a moment before struggling to find the right words.

"Have you ever looked through an unfocused telescope, only to turn the knob and make everything sharp and clear?" he asked.

Rosa nodded.

"That is what it was like for me, a few minutes ago. One moment I had all these sensations I couldn't explain swirling inside me, then the next everything made sense. The way your kisses haunted me, the fact

I wanted to deport Darius for kissing your hand—they weren't isolated sensations at all. They were my soul coming back to life."

"Just like that?" She still sounded skeptical, but she had continued leaning against him. Armando took that as progress.

"Like a bolt of lightning," he said, kissing her neck again.

She pulled away, leaving him standing in the middle of the archway by himself. "You don't believe me."

"I…"

"Or…" A second thought came to him. About how easily she brushed off his apology as his ego. "Is it that you don't care?"

So excited had he been about his revelation that he didn't stop to think that she might not share his feelings. He was ashamed of himself, although not nearly as ashamed as he was disappointed. Having come back to life, he desperately wanted her to feel the same intensity of desire and need that he felt.

Still, if she didn't, he had no choice but to respect her wishes. "I'm sorry if I've made you feel uncomfortable," he told her. "I let my enthusiasm cloud my judgment."

"No, you didn't," she said, turning. "Make me feel uncomfortable, that is. I do care. I'm not quite sure when things changed, but I care a lot."

"But?" There was no mistaking the hesitancy in her voice. As much as her proclamation made his spirits want to soar, Armando held them in check and prayed what came next wasn't rejection.

Rosa shrugged, palms up. "I don't know what to think," she said.

"Then don't think," he replied. "Just go with your heart."

"I—I don't know," Rosa replied.

He made it sound easy. *Just go with your heart.* But what if your heart was frightened and confused? She had come to terms with her feelings being one-sided, only to hear him say they weren't. How could she be sure this sudden realization wasn't a reaction to another man coveting his possession? After all, Armando was used to having her undivided attention. Who was to say that once he claimed her attention again he wouldn't lose interest? Chubby, divorced, insecure. Wasn't as if she had a bucket load of qualities to offer.

Nor had he said he loved her. He cared for her, needed her, wanted her. All wonderful words, but none of them implied he was offering his heart. For all his talk of coming to life, he was essentially in the same place as before, unable or unwilling to give her a true emotional commitment. He was simply done trying to be fair. Flattering to think his desire for her was great enough to override his sense of honor.

On the other hand, her feelings wanted to override her common sense, so maybe they were even. As she watched him close the gap between them, she felt her heartbeat quicken to match her breath.

"You do know that we're under the mistletoe yet again, don't you?"

Damn sprig of berries had quite a knack for timing, didn't it? Anticipation ran down her spine breaking what little hold common sense still had. Armando was going kiss her, and she was going to let him. She wanted to lose herself in his arms. Believe for a moment that his heart felt more than simple desire.

This time when he wrapped his arm

around her waist, she slid against him willingly, aligning her hips against his with a smile.

"Appears to be our fate," she whispered. "Mistletoe, that is."

"You'll get no complaints from me." She could hear her heart beating in her ears as his head dipped toward hers. "Merry Christmas, Rosa."

"Mer—" His kiss swallowed the rest of her wish. Rosa didn't care if she spoke another word again. She'd waited her whole life to be kissed like this. Fully and deeply, with a need she felt all the way down to her toes.

They were both breathless when the moment ended. With their foreheads resting against each other, she felt Armando smile against her lips. "Merry Christmas," he whispered again.

Rosa felt like a princess.

Behind them, a throat cleared. "I beg your pardon, Your Highness."

The voice belonged to Vittorio Mastella, head of security. He stood in the doorway as statue-like as ever, dare she say even overly so, the way his hands were glued tight against his thighs. "I've been asked to deliver a message to you."

Armando tightened his hold on her waist, clearly afraid she might flee. "If it's Father, tell him I'm not feeling well, and I will see him in the morning," he said, smiling at Rosa. "I'm in the middle of a very important discussion."

"I'm afraid it's not from your father." The way his eyes flickered between the two of him made Rosa uneasy. Whatever the message, it sounded like unwanted news.

She couldn't have been more right.

"Princess El Halwani has arrived," Vittorio announced. "She's on her way to the dining room as we speak."

CHAPTER NINE

ENTER THE BIGGEST stumbling block of all. How on earth could Rosa have forgotten about Mona, the ultimate reason for holding back her heart? At the sound of her name, she broke free of Armando's embrace. Easy enough since his grip had gone lax.

"Thank you, Vittorio," Armando replied.

From his shell-shocked expression, it appeared he had forgotten about Mona as well. Small consolation, but Rosa took it nonetheless.

Vittorio bowed in response. "Again, I'm sorry for the interruption, Your Highness."

"No need to apologize, Vittorio. Your timing was fine."

Fortuitous even, Rosa would say. This was the second time she and Armando had been stopped from kissing. Maybe the universe knew the troubles that lay ahead and had stepped in to protect them. Certainly it had saved her from heartache tonight.

Partly, anyway.

The two of them stood listening to Vittorio's receding footsteps. Armando looked as dazed as she felt. His eyes were flat and distant.

She broke the silence first. "We'd best be heading back to the dining room as well. You don't want the princess wondering where you went."

"Yes, we should," he replied in a voice as far away as the rest of him. Then he coughed. The action seemed to shake him back to life, because when he looked at her, his eyes were sharper. Apologetic. "We should talk later."

"There isn't that much to talk about," she replied. Whatever they'd been about to discover was a missed opportunity.

They were met at the dining room entrance by both King Carlos and King Omar. While Armando's father wore a concerned frown, the sultan looked ready to burst with excitement. "There you are, my friend! I wondered where you had gone to for so long."

"I was feeling under the weather," Armando replied, "and went out for some fresh air."

"With your assistant?" King Carlos asked.

"I asked Rosa if she would get me something for my stomach. Vittorio told me Mona has arrived."

"Yes!" replied Omar. "The weather finally cleared, and our pilot was able to get clearance. She is freshening up after her flight and will be back momentarily. You do look pale," the sultan noted, cocking his head. "I hope it is nothing serious. This arrangement has been plagued enough by illness. Ah, here is my daughter now."

It was like a scene in a movie. At the sound of King Omar's pronouncement, all heads turned to the far end of the room to see Princess Mona walk in.

Not walk, float. She moved like she was moving on air with the amethyst color of her gossamer gown trailing behind her. "My deepest apologies, King Carlos," she said after executing a perfect curtsy, "for arriving so late. I hope I am not disrupting your daughter's special evening."

"You can blame me," Omar said. "Mona was going to go to a hotel, but I insisted she make an appearance. She and your son were long overdue to spend time together."

"You are most right, Omar," King Carlos replied before kissing Mona's fingers. "Your presence is welcome no matter how late. I've already instructed the staff to add a setting next to Armando."

"You're too kind, Your Highness." She cast her eyes down in appropriate demureness, her eyelashes fluttering like butterfly wings.

For a woman who wasn't planning to attend, she looked breathtaking. Her dark hair was pulled back tight to give accent to her almond-shaped eyes and high cheekbones. And her skin…her complexion looked like someone had airbrushed her.

The woman turned her curtsy to Armando. "Prince Armando, I'm so pleased to see you again."

Armando nodded. "I'm glad to see you

are fully recovered. You…" He cleared his throat. "You look as lovely as I remember."

"I'm a fright from rushing to get here, but thank you for the compliment. I'm looking forward to our getting to know each other better over this next week."

"The same here." He coughed again. "Sorry. I think might need a glass of water."

"As good a cue as any to take our seats before your sister notices we are gone," King Carlos said. "Although I would say the odds are in our favor."

"They do appear very much enamored with one another," Omar noted.

"Indeed," said the king. "If we were to all go to bed right now, I am not sure they would care. In fact, we may have to tell them when dinner has ended."

Speaking of not being noticed… Rosa lagged behind as the royal quartet walked away. There was a brief moment when Armando looked back, but she purposely didn't catch his eye. Looking at him would only cause her to replay their conversation in the archway, and she felt cold and alone enough as it was.

"Hey, beautiful, I'd wondered where you'd gone. They're just about to serve the main course. Or so the forks tell me." Leaping to his feet, Darius pushed in her chair. "Everything okay with the boss man?"

She looked across the table to where Armando was introducing the princess to the rest of the guests. They made a good-looking couple, the two of them. They would make good-looking heirs as well.

"Why wouldn't it be?" she asked.

"The two of you were gone for a while. I was afraid something might have happened. Some kind of royal attack or something. We're not under attack, are we?" he whispered teasingly.

Rosa forced a smile. It wasn't Darius's fault she'd left her affinity for flirting back in the archway. "No attack. Yet," she replied. "His Highness had a problem he was trying to work out."

"Did he?"

"Turns out he forgot an important piece of information. But," she said as Mona laughed, making it her time to feel sick to her stomach, "now that he has it, I'm sure he knows what he has to do."

It was the longest meal of Armando's life. Bad enough before, when he was listening to Darius attempting to charm Rosa. But once Mona came, he was forced to be charming himself while listening to Darius. All the while wishing he was standing under the mistletoe with Rosa.

Rosa, who refused to catch his eye.

Just as well. It had been wrong of him to declare his feelings when he was obligated to Mona. Selfish and wrong. His only defense was that he'd been doing exactly what he'd advised Rosa to do: not think.

Now, as punishment for his greediness, he could spend the rest of the evening tasting Rosa's kiss. The sensation of her mouth moving under his overrode his taste buds, turning everything that passed his lips bland and lifeless. By the time dessert arrived, he wanted to toss his napkin on the table and tell everyone he was through.

He didn't, of course. One abrupt departure was enough. Besides, between his behavior and Mona's late arrival, he'd stolen the spotlight enough.

Well, he had wanted to give people something to gossip about besides Arianna's pregnancy. Sitting to his left, Mona dabbed her lips with her napkin. "Father was right," she said. "Your sister and her fiancé are very devoted to one another. No wonder your father is willing to be so…accepting…of the circumstances."

"What do you mean?"

"Please don't get me wrong," she said. "I only meant that Corinthia has a reputation for being almost as traditional and conservative as my country. That your father doesn't seem fazed by your sister doing things out of order, if you will, says something."

"The order doesn't matter. Max's devotion to Arianna is indisputable."

"She is very lucky. As you and I both know, love matches in royal marriages are rare."

Yes, they were. Yet again, he tried to catch Rosa's attention, but her profile was firmly turned toward Darius.

Armando flexed his fingers to keep from

forming a fist. A lock of hair had fallen over her eye, loosened no doubt, when they'd kissed. He wanted to comb it away from her face simply so he could run his fingers through her hair.

He wanted to do a lot of things. Apparently being haunted by her kiss wasn't enough—all his other buried urges returned as well.

Coming back to life was killing him.

"Over time…"

Mona was talking to him again. He jerked his attention back. "I'm sorry. I missed what you said."

"I was talking about royal marriages," she said. "That the absence of love in the beginning doesn't mean the marriage won't be successful. After all, if two people are compatible, there is no reason why they won't develop feelings for one another over time. Love doesn't always happen at first sight."

"No, it doesn't," Armando murmured. Sometimes love crept up on you over a period of years, disguising itself as friendship until your heart was ready.

"Especially when there are children and

mutual interests involved," Mona continued. "When two people are committed to the same goals."

"Working as a team," Armando said.

"Precisely."

That's what he and Rosa were. A perfectly matched team.

You didn't break up a perfect team.

He would tell Mona tonight that their arrangement was off. There would be a scandal, which would divert attention away from Arianna and her child's illegitimacy. That had been the point of accelerating his marriage plans in the first place. Meanwhile he would court Rosa properly.

Fingertips grazed the back of his hand, causing him to stiffen. Mona smiled apologetically. "You looked a million miles away," she said.

"I'm sorry. I was thinking about the future." One that looked bright for the first time in years.

"I'm glad to hear it," she replied, "because I have, too."

Sadly, they weren't thinking of the same future, and for that, he felt terrible. It wasn't

Mona's fault love had a bad sense of timing. "Perhaps we should talk after dinner," he said.

"I would like that," Mona replied. She looked down at their hands, which were still connected, she having left hers atop his. "I hope you don't think me too forward, but I believe you and I could do a lot of good together."

The muscles along the back of Armando's neck began to tense. "Good?" he repeated.

"Yes. The flu I caught the other week. Father told you I caught it volunteering at the hospital? He lied. What he didn't tell you was that the people of Yelgiers are suffering from a terrible health care crisis. A lot of our citizens, mostly women and children, are without decent medical attention. The fact that women are still treated as second-class citizens in many parts of the country, and are therefore seen as undeserving of care, only exacerbates the problem. So many women suffer in silence."

"Too many," Armando noted, thinking of the women at Christina's Home.

"I've been reading up on how much your

government has done these past years to improve conditions for women and children. I'm hoping that when our countries are united," she said, squeezing his hand, "our countries' combined assets will help all our people."

Our people. Armando stared at his untouched dessert, the weight of Mona's speech pressing down upon his shoulders. With a few eloquent sentences, Mona had reminded him how much was at stake. Their engagement wasn't just about them. It wasn't even about protecting his family from scandal. It was about doing what was best for his people. Corinthia was counting on him to lead them to a prosperous future. To keep them safe and healthy. And now, thanks to his agreement with Omar, so were the people of Yelgiers.

Every single candle in every single window…

If he broke off the engagement, it would mean far more than some headlines and bad blood. While they might not realize it, there were people who needed his marriage to Mona to make their lives better.

How could he walk away knowing he was failing people? His people. Mona's people. As much as he loved Rosa—and, oh, God, he did love her, more than he thought possible—he could never live with himself.

Better to settle for kisses under the mistletoe and be able to look at himself in the mirror.

He'd been right earlier. Love really did have terrible timing.

For the first time in her life, Rosa couldn't find comfort in a chocolate dessert.

"Don't tell me you're pregnant, too," Darius joked. "You've got that same green-around-the-gills look the princess used to get when she first showed up in New York."

No such luck, she thought, putting a hand to her stomach. If she were pregnant with Armando's child, she would be doing cartwheels of joy. The only thing making her green was a bad case of jealousy. Brought on by seeing Mona holding Armando's hand.

"Just indigestion," she replied.

"I hear ya," Darius replied. "That was a

lot of food. Makes me wonder what we're going to get at the wedding tomorrow."

Oh, Lord, the wedding. Maybe she could claim illness and stay home. That way she wouldn't have to face another eight hours of seeing Armando and Mona together.

The American leaned back in his chair with a satisfied sigh. "Thank goodness I've got till tomorrow night to digest everything. Otherwise, I might need some emergency tailoring on my tuxedo. Max would kill me. You sure it's indigestion?" he asked at her halfhearted laugh.

"It is." Rosa was still staring at the joined hands across the way. Whatever Mona was talking about had to be serious. Armando was frowning at his untouched plate.

"I don't know," Darius replied. "That prince of yours looks pretty green, too."

"He's not my prince," Rosa answered reflexively. Never was, but for five minutes under the mistletoe.

Now that Darius mentioned it, though, Armando did look pale. Good. Petty as it was, she wanted him to feel as terrible as she did. She also wanted Mona to trip over her floaty train and fall on her face.

No, she didn't. It wasn't the Yelgierian's fault she was beautiful and graceful and probably brilliant.

She wasn't even angry with Armando. Not much, anyway. It had been her choice to kiss him. He'd said to stop thinking, and she did. A smarter woman would have heeded her own warnings. Then again, a smarter woman wouldn't have fallen for Armando in the first place.

To think, she'd started dinner feeling empowered. The joke was on her. She was a bigger fool than even Fredo thought she was.

The wedding of Princess Arianna Santoro and Maxwell Brown, the newly named Conte de Corinth, went flawlessly. Not only did security keep the press away, but the bride's former boyfriend departed that morning on a lengthy trip to the continent. With all potential drama eliminated, the result was an intimate and beautifully romantic ceremony that even the people of Corinthia seemed content to let stay private.

Armando and his father had to be pleased. A week from now, Armando would announce his engagement, the country would be plunged into wedding fervor yet again and no one would ever remember the princess's pregnancy started before she met Max in New York.. Plus by this time next year, Mona would probably be pregnant—because she was no doubt amazingly fertile along with all her other qualities. Success all around. Long live the royal family of Corinthia.

Because it was Christmas Eve, the reception did double duty as a holiday celebration, only instead of trees, there were towers of poinsettias, each near ten feet high. People could be seen exchanging gifts by them when they weren't dancing and enjoying the wedding festivities. Seated at a table by one of the ballroom windows, Rosa triple-checked whether the decorations included mistletoe. Given her and Armando's recent track record with the plant, one could never be too careful.

There wasn't any. Meaning there was no excuse for even the most casual of kisses.

She cursed the way her heart fell.

"You should be careful. I hear there's a law in this country against outshining the bride." Darius handed her a glass of wine before helping himself to the seat next to her.

"Little chance of that, I'm afraid. Did you see Arianna?" She nodded to where the princess and her husband were posing for a photograph. Given the circumstances, Arianna had forgone a traditional gown in favor of simple pink satin, but her happy glow made her easily the most beautiful woman in the room.

"She looks good, but you're definitely a close second."

Rosa rolled her eyes. "Sounds like someone's been helping himself to the champagne."

"Sounds like someone needs to help herself to a little more." To prove his point, his added the remaining contents of his glass to hers. "Here, drink up," he said, sliding the glass toward her. "It'll make watching them a little easier."

"I don't know what you're talking about." Surely she wasn't that transparent.

Apparently she was, because the man immediately gave her a look. "Sweetheart, I'm a New York bartender. I know how to read people. In your case, it's not that hard. You've been watching the guy since last night's main course."

No sense pretending she didn't know what he meant. Directly across the dance floor, Armando and Mona were talking to her father, Omar. Mona was the one dangerously close to upstaging the bride. Her strapless gown looked sewn onto her body.

She paled compared to Armando, though. Both he and his father were in full regalia for the wedding, navy blue uniforms complete with sash and sword. He looked like he belonged on a white charger.

"For crying out loud, you're staring at him right now," Darius said. "Damn good thing I don't have self-esteem issues."

"I'm sorry. I don't mean to be rude. I…"

"Got a thing for the guy?"

Rosa felt her cheeks burn. Quickly, she grabbed her wine and swallowed. "I'm afraid it's complicated."

"I know. I met her last night. What's her deal, anyway?"

Rosa told him.

"Fiancée, huh? Then why were you two sneaking off last night? I told you, I'm observant," he added when she gasped.

Because Armando got jealous and said he wanted her. He kissed her like she'd never been kissed before, and probably never would be again. He let her pretend for a moment that a woman like her could be a princess, and now she was sitting at a wedding angry at her own foolishness.

"I told you," she said. "It's complicated."

"I bet. Complicated is why I'm glad I'm single. Come on." He stood up and held out his hand. "Let's fox-trot."

Rosa shook her head. "I don't think…"

"You really want to sit here looking like a sad chipmunk all night, or do you want him to see you enjoying yourself next time he looks in your direction?"

Rosa looked over to see Mona place a proprietary hand on Armando's arm. The woman certainly didn't waste time marking her territory. "There's a good chance I'll step on your toes."

"Good, that makes two of us."

Darius, it turned out, was a worse dancer than she was. By the second song, they were both laughing over how much they were tripping up the other. Rosa had to admit, it felt good to make mistakes and laugh about them. Made her forget her heartache for a little while.

That was, until a familiar hand tapped Darius on the shoulder. "May I?" Armando asked. His eyes, as well as his request, were directed at her.

Rosa could feel Darius tightening his grip in an effort to protect her. "It's all right," she told him. Actually, it was probably a mistake, but the chance to be in Armando's arms was too great a temptation to pass up.

"You two seem to be enjoying yourselves," Armando said when she stepped into his arms. "I'm sorry I had to interrupt." Rosa bristled at his barely disguised jealousy. What made him think he had any right?

"Isn't that the point of a wedding? To enjoy yourself?"

"I didn't mean that the way it sounded," he replied. He twirled their bodies toward a far end of the dance floor. "That's a lie. I meant it exactly as it sounded. It killed me to see you in his arms."

"Really? Because watching you with Mona is a picnic."

Her jab hit its mark, because he immediately winced. "You're right. I have no business saying anything, and I'm sorry."

"So am I," she replied. If these were to be the only moments Armando held her, she didn't want to waste them fighting. It was because the position reminded her too much of last night, and the memories were too raw to handle politely. She ached for him to close the distance between their bodies. A few inches, that was all. Enough for her to rest her head on his shoulder and pretend the rest of the world didn't exist.

Instead, the song ended. She started to step away, but Armando tightened his grip on her waist. "One more dance," he said. "There's something I need to say."

"Armando…" He was going to talk about Mona and obligations and all the other topics she wanted to forget.

"Please, Rosa."

Whatever made her think she had a chance? Letting out a breath, she relaxed into his touch. "You know I can never say no to you."

"I know," he replied.

While he spoke, his gaze traced a line along her cheek, performing the caress he couldn't do by hand. Rosa's insides cried for the touch.

They danced in silence for what felt like forever. Finally, just when she was ready to say something, Armando spoke. "Do you know what I did last night?" he asked.

She shook her head.

"I couldn't sleep, so I counted the lights I could see from my bedroom window. Seven hundred fourteen. In that one patch of space. Do you know how many there are in the entire country? One point two million."

"Oh, 'Mando." She knew where this was going.

"Never have I resented so many lights," he said, gazing past her.

"That's not true. You don't resent them," she replied. "You love them."

Still looking past her shoulder, Armando sighed. "You're right. I wish I did hate them, though. I wish I didn't care what happened to any of them."

He pulled his gaze back to her, and she saw that the perpetual melancholy that clouded his eyes was twice as thick. "I do, though. Dammit, I do."

"I'm glad." Yes, a selfish part of her wanted him not to care, but it was Armando's love for his people that made him who he was.

"She wants to improve medical care. Mona. That's what she wants to do when we're married. Improve medical care in both countries. There will be thousands more candles to look after."

She could feel the responsibility pushing down upon him. Suddenly Rosa understood. He was backed into a corner. Choose duty and save lives. Choose for himself and fail two countries. Whatever anger she might still have began to fade. "You're doing the right thing," she told him. Like he always did. The responsible young boy who looked out for his sister on a bigger scale. "Corinthia—and Yelgiers—are lucky to have a leader who cares so much."

"Perhaps." He didn't look convinced. He looked...sad. "I had no right to kiss you, Rosa. It was wrong."

"Don't say that."

"But it's true. I knew I had obligations, and yet, like a selfish bastard, I went after what I wanted anyway. Who knows what would have happened if Vittorio hadn't interrupted us?"

They both knew what would have happened.

"How does that make me any different than Fredo?" he asked.

His self-loathing had gone too far. Halting her steps, she touched her fingers to his lips to silence him. "You are nothing like Fredo."

He smiled and kissed her fingertips. "Aren't I, though? You deserve better."

Except there wasn't anyone better. If the feelings in her heart were to be believed, there never would be. "In case you didn't notice, there were two people kissing," she told him. "We both ignored our common sense."

Armando shook his head. "Dear, sweet Rosa. You still won't admit you are a victim."

"Because I'm not a victim." Not this time. "Last night, you made me feel more special in five minutes than I had ever felt in my entire life. I would trade all the common sense in the world for that."

"If I could, I would make you feel special every day. You deserve nothing less."

"Neither do you."

He smiled sadly. "But apparently I do."

The song ended, but they had stopped dancing long ago in favor of standing in each other's arms. Rosa's first assessment was right—it was much too similar to last night's embrace. When Armando's eyes dropped to her mouth, common sense was again poised to disappear.

"I love you, Rosa. I'm sorry I didn't come to my senses sooner."

He pulled away, leaving her to shudder from the withdrawal. She was still in a daze. Did he say he loved her? *Loved?*

The sound of a spoon against crystal rang across the ballroom. King Carlos had stepped up to the front of the room.

"Ladies and gentlemen, might I have your attention?" Instantly, the ballroom went silent.

"Arianna asked me to refrain from formal toasts and speeches during last evening's dinner, and as you all know, while I rule Corinthia, she rules me." Low laughter rippled through the crowd. Rosa sneaked a look at Armando and saw he hadn't cracked a smile. "However, I cannot let this evening end without saying a few words, not as your king, but as a father."

The king's smile softened. "This family has seen its share of loss over the past few years. My wife. Princess Christina." At the sound of her sister's name, Rosa looked to the floor.

"But now, as I look at the faces around the room and I see the smile on my daughter's beautiful face, my heart is filled with so much hope. Hope for new beginnings. Hope for the next generation, and the generations of Santoros to come. I've never been prouder of my children. Just as I am proud of my newest son, Maxwell. I hope also to add a new daughter soon as well." Everyone but she and Armando looked in Mona's direction. Armando kept his attention on his father, while Rosa lifted her eyes to watch Armando.

"I am getting older," the king continued. "Older and tired. There may come a day in the future when I decide to step down."

A gasp could be heard in the crowd. King Carlos held up a hand. "No need to be upset. I'm not worried. Because I see the people who will be taking my place, and I couldn't be more pleased."

The rest of his toast was a flurry of well wishes for Arianna and Max. At least that was what she assumed. Armando had turned to her, and she found herself transfixed by his blue stare. *I'm sorry*, his eyes were saying. *I have no choice.*

All Rosa could hear were the words she'd convinced herself he wasn't going to say. *I love you.* A lifetime and she wouldn't hear three more beautiful words.

She loved him, too.

What was she going to do come Monday? And the Monday after that? What about when Armando announced his engagement? Knowing he loved her might sound wonderful today, but how was she going to face him day in and day out when he belonged to someone else?

Simple answer was, she couldn't. Not without the self-esteem she'd worked so hard to rebuild crumbling into pieces again.

There was only one answer.

CHAPTER TEN

"ALL ARE ONE…" The last words of the Corinthian national anthem rose from the crowd gathered below the balcony. Arianna and Max had been officially presented as a royal couple.

Leaving Father and the happy couple to greet their well wishers, Armando stepped back inside. There was only so much joy a man could take, and he had met his limit.

He was happy for his sister, truly he was, but if he had to watch her and Max gaze into each other's eyes a second longer, he would scream.

A few moments alone in the empty gallery would clear his head. Then he would be ready to tackle the rest of Christmas Day. Mona and her father were joining the celebration. Another day being reminded of the hole he'd dug himself into. At least he'd apologized to Rosa, taking that guilt off his shoulders. Somewhat. He doubted he would ever be completely guilt-free.

Because part of him would never regret kissing her.

To his surprise, Rosa was in the gallery when he entered, studying one of the china cabinets. One look and his energy returned, even if she was wearing one of those ridiculous long blazers he hated. He hadn't expected to see her for a few days. He'd wanted to—oh, Lord, had he wanted to—but common sense had made a rare appearance and suggested otherwise. If he went to her apartment, he would be tempted to pull her into his arms. Much like he was tempted right now.

When she saw him, she smiled. "Merry Christmas," she greeted.

Something wasn't right. He could tell by the sound of her voice. "The crowd sounds thrilled with their princess's new husband" she said.

"So it would seem. If I were a gambling man, I would bet Max embraces his royal role very quickly."

"That would be good for Corinthia."

"Yes." That was what mattered, wasn't it? The best for Corinthia? "What are you doing here?" he asked. The question came out more accusatory than he meant. "I thought you were helping out at the shelter this afternoon."

"I wanted to come by and give you your Christmas present." She pointed to a wrapped box on the seat of a nearby chair.

Armando walked over and fingered the cheerful silver bow. He didn't know what to say.

"Don't worry, it's not booby-trapped, I promise," she said. A halfhearted attempt to shake off the awkward atmosphere.

It wasn't booby trapping that had him off balance—it was wondering whether he deserved the kindness.

"My gift for you is under the tree upstairs," he said. A gold charm bracelet marking moments from their friendship.

"You can give it to me later. I can't stay long, and I want to see you open yours. Go ahead," she urged.

He peeled back the gift wrap. It was an

antique wood statue of Babbo Natale. The colors were fading, but the carving itself was flawless.

"I found it in a shop outside the city. The owner thought he was handmade around the turn of the century. Silly, I know, but what else do you get the guy who has everything? You've already got plenty of ties," she added with a self-conscious laugh.

"Don't apologize," Armando told her. "It's beautiful. Truly handcrafted pieces are hard to find."

"When I saw him, I thought he looked a little like you do when you're wearing the costume. Around the eyes."

He turned the statue over in his hands. "I'll take your word for it." It didn't matter if the statue resembled him or the queen of England. She could have given him a paper doll and he would have treasured the piece. Because it came from her.

He longed to pull her into a hug. "Thank you. I love it." *And you.*

"I…" All of a sudden, she stopped talking and pivoted abruptly so she stood with her back turned to him. Something was definitely wrong, he thought, his shoulders stiffening. "I thought it would make a good memory to share with your child," she continued. "About those times you played Santa Claus at the shelter."

"You talk as if I won't be there anymore." That was never going to happen. The shelter and its mission were too important to him. More so now that he knew her story.

"Not you," Rosa replied, her back still turned. "Me."

Her? Armando's stomach dropped. "What are you talking about?"

When she didn't reply right away, he reached for her shoulder. To hell with not touching her. "What do you mean, you?"

"I-I'm leaving."

No. She couldn't be. Armando's hand fell away short of its goal. "You're not going to be my assistant anymore?"

"I can't." Finally, she turned around. When he saw her face, Armando almost wished he hadn't. Her eyes were damp and shining. "I can't come to work every day and see you. It's too dangerous."

"I don't understand." His mind was too

stuck on her resignation to make sense of anything else. "Dangerous for whom?"

"Me," she replied.

She started to pace. Rosa being the one to mark paths on the carpeting for a change would be amusing if the circumstances were different. "I thought about what you said last night, about my deserving better," she said.

"You do. You deserve—"

She cut him off. "I know. Surprisingly. Fredo convinced me I would never deserve better than dirt, and for a long time I believed it."

He watched as a tear dripped down her cheek. "Then you said you loved me. Loved. And I started thinking, if a man like you thinks he loves me..."

"I do love you," he said, rushing toward her.

"Don't." With her hands in front of her chest, she shook her head. "This is why I have to quit."

"You don't want to be near me."

"Don't you understand? I want to be near you too much. You're marrying someone else, 'Mando.

"And I get it," she said when he opened his mouth to tell her she was—she would always be—his first choice. "I understand the responsibility you feel toward your country, and why you need to keep your word. I love your sense of honor.

"But if I stay, I'll be tempted to be with you no matter what the circumstances, and I can't be the woman you love on the side. I worked too hard on being myself again."

She was shaking by the time she finished. With tears staining her cheeks. It killed him to stand there when every fiber of his being wanted to steal her away to a place where they could be together. It killed him, but he knew it was what Rosa wanted. Just as he knew he couldn't fight her leaving.

"What will I do without you?" he asked instead.

"You survived without me for years, 'Mando. I'm sure you'll survive again." Armando hated to think the last smile he'd see on her face would be this sad facsimile that didn't reach her eyes.

"Where will you go? What will you do?"

"I don't know yet. Right now, I'm going

to focus on celebrating Christmas. I'll figure out the rest tomorrow."

"You survived once, you'll survive again," he repeated softly.

"Exactly." Her fingers were shaking as she wiped her cheeks. "Merry Christmas, Your Highness. Happy New Year, too."

Not without her in it.

With Babbo Natale cradled in his arms, he stood alone in the gallery and listened to the sound of the elevator doors closing. "Don't go," he whispered.

But like her sister had three years before, Rosa left anyway.

"Was that Rosa I saw getting on the elevator?" Arianna asked. She strolled in with Max and Father trailing behind. Her face pink from the cold, she shrugged off her coat and draped it over the arm of a chair. "I wish I'd known she was coming by. I have a Christmas present for her. Is that what Rosa gave you?" she asked, noting the wood carving. "It's lovely."

"What's lovely?" Max asked.

"The carving Rosa gave Max," Arianna replied.

"I'm not surprised," Father said. "She's always had impeccable taste." He went on to tell Max a story about an ornament Armando's mother bought the year Arianna was born. Armando continued to watch the doorway in case Rosa decided to return.

"She was determined to find the perfect ornament to mark Arianna's first Christmas. We must have gone to every shop, craftsman and artist in Corinthia, and nothing was good enough. If I'd thought I could learn fast enough, I would have taken up glassblowing myself so she could design her own. It has to be perfect for our baby, she kept saying."

Armando had already heard the ending. How his mother finally found the ornament in a gift shop in Florence, and it turned out to have been made by a Corinthian expatriate who insisted on giving the ornament as a gift for the new princess. The reverence in his father's voice as he spoke was at near worship proportions. His words practically dripped with love.

Armando's head started to hurt.

"I know she would be thrilled to look

down and see the ornament on your tree, for your child."

"I'm only sorry she isn't here," he heard Arianna say with a sniff.

"We can only hope she is watching right now, happy and proud of both of you."

Would she be proud, Armando wondered. Would she be happy to know her eldest son had let the woman he loved walk away?

He worked up the courage to turn around, only to find a portrait of marital bliss. Max stood behind Arianna, arms wrapped around her to rest his hands on her bump. His father stood a few feet away, beaming with paternal approval. He tried to imagine himself in the picture, his arms around a pregnant Mona. Imagine himself content.

All he could see was Rosa's back as she walked away.

It wasn't fair. Father had said last night, their family had seen its share of dark days. Armando had buried his wife, for God's sake. He turned off a machine and watched her take her last breath! Did that moment truly mean he would never have love again? If that was the case, then why wake his heart up? Why torment him by having him fall in love with Rosa after he'd agreed to marry King Omar's daughter? Wouldn't it be better to keep his heart buried? Or was loving and losing another woman his punishment for some kind of cosmic crime?

"Armando!" Arianna was staring at him with wide eyes. "What is wrong with you?"

"You're choking Santa Claus," Max added.

He looked down and saw he had a white-knuckle grip on the statue. A more delicate piece would have snapped in two.

"I…" He dropped the figurine on the closest table like it was on fire. Babbo landed off balance and fell over, his wooden sack of toys hitting the table first with a soft thud.

Arianna appeared by his side, reaching past him to set the statue upright. "Are you all right?" she asked him. "You've been acting odd since late last night. Did something happen between you and Rosa?"

"Why would you ask that?"

"Because you and she are usually joined at the hip, and the past few days…"

"I have a headache is all," he snapped.

The air in the gallery was feeling close. He needed space. "I've got to get some air."

Of course he would end up sitting in the archway, under the mistletoe. Trying to put your head on straight always worked best in a room full of memories. Sinking down on the next to last step, he scrubbed his face with his hands, looking to erase the night of the concert from his brain. Instead, he saw Rosa, her face bathed in golden light.

What was he going to do? Leaning back, he stared up at the mistletoe sprig. "You have been nothing but trouble, do you know that?"

If the berries had a retort, they kept it to themselves. Bastards.

A flash of gold and green caught his eye. A few feet to his left, he noticed an angel perched near the top of the tree. Unlike the other ornaments, which were ornate almost to the point of ostentation, the angel was simple and made of felt with a mound of golden hair surrounding her face. He really must be losing his mind; the way the angel was hung, it looked like she was watching him. "What do you think I should do, angel? Do I do the honorable thing and keep my promise to Mona? Or do I go against everything I've ever been taught to run after Rosa?"

Nothing.

That's what he thought. As if a Christmas ornament would know any more than a branch of mistletoe.

Why then did he feel as though the answer was right there, waiting for him to see it? "Why did Christina have to die in the first place?" he asked the angel. "Life would be so much easier if she had just taken the curve a little slower. I wouldn't have needed to enter an agreement with King Omar because I wouldn't need a wife."

And Rosa would still be with Fredo. Unacceptable. As much as he had loved Christina, he would never bring her back if it meant leaving Rosa married and fearful. Christina wouldn't want to come back under those circumstances.

But she would tell you to follow your heart. That life is too short to waste time feeling angry and unhappy. Not when happi-

ness is within your reach. All you have to do is to be brave enough to take a chance. To sneak out after dark and turn on the Christmas lights.

To leave the abusive husband. If Rosa could be brave enough to walk away from Fredo, if the other women could walk away from worse, then surely he could summon up enough bravery to be happy.

"Armando! Are you here?"

Looked like he would be tested sooner than he thought. "In the archway, Father."

"I should have known." King Carlos appeared at the top of the opposite stairs. "I swear you are as bad as your sister regarding these lights," he said as he navigated the steps.

"It's too cold to go outside," Armando told him. "This is the next best thing."

"You are aware you are sitting under the mistletoe?"

"Believe me, I know. Damn plant is following me."

His father chuckled. "You, my son, might be the first person I have ever heard complain about kissing traditions. Or is it a more specific problem?" he asked, settling himself on the step as well. "Your sister is right. You've been out of sorts for a few days now. Did something happen?"

"You could say that," Armando replied. He stared at his palms. Maybe one of the lines had the words he needed to explain. "Did you mean what you said last night? About being proud of Arianna and me?"

Whatever his father had been expecting, that wasn't it. He leaned back a little so he could see Armando's face. "Of course I did. You make me immensely proud."

Would he still feel that way once Armando finished—that was the question. "Even if I dishonored Corinthia?"

"Considering your sister married a man who is not the father of her child, it would be hypocritical of me, don't you think? Besides, I doubt there's anything you could do that would dishonor Corinthia too much."

"Don't be so sure."

His father paused as what Armando said sank in. "What have you done?"

"More like what I can't do," Armando replied and looked up from his hand. He didn't need a love or life line to tell him what needed to be said. "I can't marry Mona."

"I see." There was another pause. "And why can't you?"

"Because I'm in love with someone else." He laid out the entire story, from why he contacted King Omar in the first place to his goodbye to Rosa a short time earlier. When he finished, he went back to studying his palms. "I know we're responsible for every light in Corinthia. I know that backing out of this arrangement means dishonoring our reputation and making an enemy out an important economic ally, but I just can't.

"It's selfish, but I'm tired of being unhappy, Father," he said, staring at the shadows flickering along the wall. "It's been three years of not being among the living. I need to live again."

By this point, he'd been expecting his father's silence, so it was a surprise when his father responded immediately. "Every light in Corinthia? Sounds like someone spent time with his grandfather."

He reached over and patted Armando's knee, something he hadn't done in Armando's childhood. "My father was a good man, but some of his advice could be heavy-handed. If I had known he was putting such notions in your head when you were young… Apparently I've failed you as well."

"No, you didn't," Armando said, shifting his weight to face him. "You have been an exemplary king…"

"And a mediocre father," he replied. "I wallowed in my grief and, as a result, taught you by example. Of course you should be happy, Armando. You can't lead a country if you're angry and bitter. If Rosa is the woman who will make you happy, embrace her."

Armando planned to. He took a deep breath. Perhaps his father had a point. Having made his decision, he no longer felt the pressing weight on his shoulders. Like on the night of the rehearsal dinner, the bits and pieces kicking around his head had solidified, making his thoughts clear. He could breathe.

"Omar is going to be furious," he said. Mona, too. And deservedly so.

"Omar is also pragmatic. His main concern is helping his people. If we offer economic aid, I think he and Mona will be willing to swallow their hurt pride. Although I wouldn't expect an invitation to stay at the Yelgierian palace any time soon."

If that was the only fallout, Armando would live. "I would like to start an initiative as well to encourage Corinthian and other EU doctors to set up practice in Yelgiers. From what Mona says, a dearth of doctors is one of their most pressing concerns."

"We'll make it a priority," his father replied. "Now, what are you doing sitting under a mistletoe with me? Don't you have a future princess to collect?"

Yes, he did. With his cheek muscles aching from the grin on his face, Armando jumped to his feet.

"Armando!" his father called when he reached the door. "Merry Christmas."

Impossibly, Armando's grin grew even wider. "Merry Christmas, Father."

Rosa was trying. She was serving food and reminding herself that her life could be a lot worse. She had her brain. She was strong and capable. Moreover, while she might be alone, Armando loved her. Wanted, needed and loved. She should take solace in the fact she was special enough to win the heart of the crown prince.

"I'd rather have Armando."

"Are you talking to your imaginary friend, Miss Rosa?"

Daniela, she who started everything by spotting the first mistletoe, yanked on her blazer. "I have an imaginary friend, too," she said. "His name is Boco. He's a talking elephant. Is your friend an elephant, too?"

"No," said Rosa, embarrassed to be asked about her imaginary friend. "She's an angel named Christina."

"Like the name of this place?"

"That's right. She's been helping me make sense of a very confusing problem."

"Is it helping?" Daniela asked.

"Not yet," Rosa replied. "But we'll keep trying." Broken hearts were never solved in one day. And when the person you loved had also been the center of your life…she suspected she'd be trying to sort things out for a very long time.

"Maybe cake would help," Daniela said. "When my mama needs to think, she always eats cake. And ice cream."

"Your mother is a very smart woman." Though in this case, cake would only make matters worse. She'd already eaten her weight in Christmas cookies.

Sending the little girl back to play with the other children, Rosa stole a couple more cookies and made her way to the rear picture window. In the distance, Mount Cornier's snow-covered peak had been swallowed by clouds. She bit a cookie and imagined her sister's spirit sitting on a fluffy white cushion, watching over her legacy.

Holidays and heartache made her overly poetic.

If Christina was watching, the least she could do was tell her what to do next, since Rosa didn't know. In some ways, she was worse off than when she left Fredo. Then, she'd had Armando. This time she would have to lean on herself. Maybe she would go to the continent and find a job there. Or America. She didn't care so long as she could start fresh.

And someday forget Armando.

Maybe.

If she didn't—couldn't—forget him, she knew she would still survive. She wasn't the same woman who had scurried away from Fredo thinking she was a fat, ugly lump of clay. Oh, she still had days…but there were also days when she felt good about herself. The fact she made the choice to walk away from Armando said she was stronger.

In time, she would be all right. Sad. Lonely. But all right.

"If only you could make my heart stop feeling like it was tearing in two," she whispered to the glass.

"Ho, ho, ho! *Buon Natale!*"

The entire shelter burst into high-pitched squeals. "Babbo!"

It couldn't be. They must have hired a professional impersonator for the day, as a surprise for the kids.

The director hadn't mentioned anything to her, though.

"Is everyone having a good Christmas?"

Uncanny. They even sounded alike. She looked in the glass hoping to catch a reflection, but it was too bright out. All she could see was a darkened silhouette in costume.

"Babbo needs your help, boys and girls."

This was silly. Armando was not at the shelter playing Babbo. As soon as she turned around she would see that the person…

Was Armando.

Why? He was dressed in costume and surrounded by children. "There's a very special person whose present Babbo forgot to deliver," he was telling them in his boisterous Babbo voice, "and I'm afraid she thinks I decided to give her present to another girl. It's really important I find her, boys and girls, so I can tell her that I would never pick someone else. That she's the most important person in the world to Babbo. In fact, Babbo cares about her so much that he wants her to come back to the North Pole with him."

Throughout his speech, Rosa moved closer. Spotting her, he dropped his voice back to normal. "Her name's Rosa," he said. "Do you know where I can find her?"

"Right there!" the children screamed, two dozen index fingers pointing in her direction.

Rosa was too stunned to breathe. "What are you doing?" she whispered.

"What do you think I am doing?" Armando said. "I've come to bring you back home where you belong." He reached through the throng to catch her fingertips. "I love you, Rosa."

Beautiful as those words were to hear, they were still only words. "I told you, Ar—Babbo. I can't stay at the North Pole." Out of the corner of her eye, she saw the children watching intently and lowered her voice to a whisper. "It hurts too much."

"But you don't understand," he whispered back. "Mona's gone. Come with me." Grabbing her hand, he led her to the shelter's lobby and closed the community room door. "I told Mona I couldn't marry her."

She had to have heard wrong. "What about your agreement with King Omar? You gave him your word."

"It's a long story. What matters is I love you and I don't want to be with anyone else."

Rosa couldn't believe what she was hearing. It was too unreal. "Are you saying that you damaged relations with one of your closest allies for me?"

"When you put it that way...yes." He pulled off his hat and beard, leaving only his disheveled self. His beautiful, disheveled self. "I would do it again, too. Are you crying?"

"Like a newborn baby." All those years married to Fredo, believing she wasn't anyone special. How wrong she had been. Armando made her feel beyond special. Not because he'd nearly created an international incident on her behalf, or tracked her down dressed like Santa Claus, although both were amazingly romantic.

No, the reason he made her feel special was in his eyes. They were shining as clear and bright as a summer's day without a trace of melancholy to be found. He was happy being with her, and that was all she needed. "I love you," she told him.

Her reward was an even brighter shine. "Does that mean you'll come back with me to the North Pole?"

"Absolutely, Babbo. Right after you kiss me under the mistletoe."

"Forget the mistletoe," he said, tossing the beard over his shoulder. Rosa gasped as he pulled her into his arms and dipped her low. "All I need is you."

New Year's Eve

"Five minutes left in the year. Will you be sad to see it end?"

Rosa took one of the glasses of champagne Armando was carrying. "Yes," she said. "And no. I'll be sorry to see December end. For all the ups and downs, it turned out to be a pretty wonderful month."

"The last week certainly was." Armando gave her a champagne-flavored kiss that quickly deepened. "Have I mentioned how glad I am that we decided to skip a formal courtship?" he asked, lips continuing to tease hers.

"Well, it did seem a little silly, considering…"

"Mmm, considering," he said, kissing her again. What they were discovering was the intimacy that came from being friends before becoming lovers. There was a level of trust that made everything they shared feel deeper. Of course, the fact Armando was an amazingly enthusiastic lover didn't hurt, either.

"You know what else I'll miss," Rosa said, turning in his arms. "Once Epiphany passes, this will become a plain old archway again."

They were in their archway now, preferring to ring in the new year alone rather than in a ballroom full of dignitaries.

Armando kissed her temple. "If you'd like, I can insist the trees stay up by royal decree."

"Is this the same royal decree where you're going to ban the use of fake Babbo beards?"

"The fibers give me a rash."

"My poor baby. Too sensitive for synthetic fibers." She snuggled closer. "As much as I'll miss the decorations, they need to go. How else will they stay special?" Christmas decorations weren't like the man with his arms around her—Armando woke up being special.

While she woke up feeling like the luckiest woman in the world.

"Besides," she told him, "we still have tonight."

"Which switches to tomorrow in less than two minutes," he replied.

A brand-new year. Given how wonderfully this year was ending, Rosa couldn't imagine what the next year had in store. As far as she was concerned, she had everything she could want sitting next to her with his arms wrapped around her waist. She loved Armando, and he loved her. What could be better?

"Do you realize," she said, pausing to take a drink, "that if we hadn't gotten our act together, you would be announcing your engagement to Mona at this very moment?"

"You're right—I did plan to be engaged by New Year's, didn't I?"

"That was before." Armando's breaking the engagement to date his assistant turned out to be scandal enough to push Arianna's pregnancy out of the papers completely. Fortunately, Mona and King Omar, while hurt, didn't hold too big a grudge. Hard to be angry at a country that was funding doctors' relocation efforts.

"There is still the matter of my producing an heir, though," Armando said, shifting his weight.

"That can be arranged," Rosa said with a smile.

"Very amusing. If you don't mind, I would like to establish my family in the proper order. Marriage, then heirs. What do you think?"

"I think that's a very logical…" Armando had moved to his knee. In his hand was the most beautiful diamond Rosa had ever seen. "Are you—" She couldn't finish the sentence; her heart was stuck in her throat.

"I am," he whispered with a nod. "Rosa Lamberti, would you do me the honor of becoming my wife?"

She never did say the word *yes*. Instead, Rosa threw her arms around his neck and kissed him until there was no doubt as to her answer. "I would be honored," she told him.

Down the hall, the crowd began chanting a countdown to midnight. Rosa and Armando didn't care. Their time was already here.

* * * * *

*If you loved Rosa and Armando's story,
find out where it all started with*
CHRISTMAS BABY FOR THE PRINCESS
the first book in Barbara Wallace's festive
ROYAL HOUSE OF CORINTHIA *duet,
available now!*

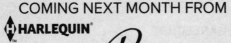

SPECIAL EXCERPT FROM

HARLEQUIN®

Romance

When Eloise Miller finds herself thrown into the role of
maid of honor at the wedding of the year, her plans to
stay away from the gorgeous best man are scuppered!

Read on for a sneak preview of
SLOW DANCE WITH THE BEST MAN,
the first book in **THE WEDDING OF THE YEAR** duet
by *Sophie Pembroke*.

Maid of honor for Melissa Sommers. How on earth had
this happened? And the worst part was—

"Sounds like we'll be spending even more time
together." Noah's voice was warm, deep and far too close
to her ear.

Eloise sighed. That. That was the worst thing. Because
the maid of honor was expected to pair up with the best
man, and that would not make her resolution to stay away
from Noah Cross any easier at all.

She turned and found him standing directly behind
her, close enough that if she'd stepped back an inch or
two she'd have been in his arms. Suddenly she was glad
he'd alerted her to his presence with his words.

She shifted farther away and tried to look like a
professional, instead of a teenager with a crush. Looking
up at him, she felt the strange heat flush over her skin
again at his gorgeousness. Then she focused, and realized
he was frowning.

HREXP1216

"Apparently so," she agreed. "But I'm sure I'll be far too busy with all the wedding arrangements—"

"Oh, I doubt it," Noah interrupted, but he still didn't sound entirely happy about the idea, which surprised her. Perhaps she'd misread his flirting earlier. Maybe he really was like that with everyone, and now that the reality of having to spend time with her had set in, he was less keen on the idea. "Melissa has quite the packed schedule for the wedding party, you know. She's right—you're going to have to find someone to take over most of your job here."

Eloise sighed. She did know. She'd helped Laurel plan it after all.

And now that she thought about it, every last bit of the schedule involved the maid of honor and the best man being together.

Noah smiled, a hint of the charm he'd exhibited earlier showing through despite the frown, and Eloise's heart beat twice in one moment as she accepted the inevitable.

She was doomed.

She had the most ridiculous crush on a man who clearly found her a minor inconvenience.

And—even worse—the whole world was going to be watching, laughing at her pretending that she could live in this world of celebrities, mocking her for thinking she could ever be pretty enough, funny enough...just *enough* for Noah Cross.

Make sure to read
SLOW DANCE WITH THE BEST MAN
by Sophie Pembroke. Available January 2017 wherever Harlequin® Romance books and ebooks are sold.

www.Harlequin.com

HREXP1216

Reading Has Its Rewards

Earn **FREE BOOKS!**

Register at **Harlequin My Rewards** and submit your Harlequin purchases from wherever you shop to earn points for free books and other exclusive rewards.

Plus submit your purchases from now till May 30th for a chance to win a $500 Visa Card*.

Visit **HarlequinMyRewards.com** today

MYR16R1